THE ENFORCER'S REDEMPTION

ARIANA COOPER

Copyright © 2025 by Ariana Cooper

All rights reserved.

No part of this book may be reproduced in any form or by any electronic or mechanical means, including information storage and retrieval systems, without written permission from the author, except for the use of brief quotations in a book review.

❦ Created with Vellum

ALSO BY ARIANA COOPER

Series: Sins of the O'Rourke Empire

The Chief's Captive || The Enforcer's Redemption

Series: Executive Arrangements

Billionaire Boss's Fake Fiancée || Single Dad's Second Chance || Billionaire Boss's One Night Stand

Series: Midnight Holiday Affairs

His Off-Limits Christmas Gift || A Christmas Bargain || Christmas with the Baby Daddy

Standalone's

Never Forget You || Office Heat

BLURB

Fifteen years of spilled blood earned me my reputation as Dublin's most ruthless enforcer.

One rule kept me alive—never show mercy... until she dared to cross my path.

Sweet little Isla O'Connor, barely twenty-two, with innocent eyes and a thief's heart.

Her father's debt demands an O'Rourke brother between her thighs.

They gave her to me—the most dangerous choice they could have made.

She fights me like a hellcat, but those whimpers in the dark tell a different story.

Each night she surrenders, every mark on her skin screams my ownership.

Then she vanishes on our wedding day carrying a secret that will shake two empires.

They took my queen, not knowing she bears the heir to Ireland's darkest throne.

Dublin's underworld will drown in blood before I let them sell what's mine.

The princess they stole will return as my queen.

And this time, I'll make sure she wears my chains with pleasure.

Author's Note: This sinful Irish Mafia romance features an age-gap enforcer who knows how to use his handcuffs, forced marriage, a forbidden pregnancy, and a bodyguard who takes his protection duties to the bedroom. Some sins are worth committing.

1

DECLAN

Sweat beads on Aisling O'Connor's forehead. It isn't just the temperature either, though we crank the thermostat for moments like this—make them think they're going crazy with how hot it is. Her pale skin and the way her hands continuously wring in her lap reveal her unease. She's not the crying type—that's a good thing. Ronan doesn't like criers., and she's in a lot of hot water.

"So he couldn't just come to my office and bitch at me?" Aisling's a beautiful woman, feisty temper though. She's just like her father, a man we've had some pretty serious business dealings with for years. If he knows what his daughter's been up to, he's never shown it.

The car bumps over potholes. I readjust in my seat, watching out the window but stealing glances at the accountant. She's playing it cool, pretending she hasn't been skimming from our enemies for the past few years. If she could get control of that sweating and the hand fidgeting, she'd be a natural in this business.

"That's not how he works." The car is quiet, Nicholas silently chauffeuring us to my brother's home, from where he runs the family. It isn't the first time I've been sent out to lay down the law, just the first time I've had to do it within the family.

"Well, I have work to do, so if you don't mind, could we go faster? I want to get this over with." Her lip twitches—her tell. She knows she's being called in to be confronted. I have to admire her grit, especially in the face of the gun barrel she's staring down.

"We work in his timing, O'Connor. You know that. And you should watch your tone when speaking with him." I flick a glance at her scowl. She readjusts herself on the leather seat and squares her shoulders as she stares out the opposite window.

My brother isn't an easy man to please, and he's not the easiest to upset, either. Unlike my father, Ronan has a very even keel. He runs this family with the same iron grip, but that iron grip also hedges in his emotional reactions. He's so hard to read, I can't even tell Ms. O'Connor what her fate might be. We only just buried the enemy. Ro won't take kindly to her rekindling the fires we just extinguished when we took out our strongest enemy.

The car rolls to a stop outside Ronan's home. Since bringing a feminine touch into his home, things have changed here too. I step out of the car and hold the door open for Aisling to get out of the car. The topiary by the front door has been trimmed, the bloodstains washed from the concrete out front. Things are getting back to normal around here.

Aisling's eyes sweep up over the front of the massive home. She has a determined expression, eyes fixed and wide, jaw set. Her lip still twitches and her hands tug on the hem of her suit jacket. She's intimidated, and she should be. Fucking with men of Ronan's caliber is dangerous. Fucking with his enemies is even more dangerous.

"Well, go on," I tell her, nudging her. She takes a few hesitant steps, her heels clicking on the pavement. It's no secret the bloodbath that went down here. I'm sure she's heard the stories. I shut the door and let my palm ride the small of her back while I guide her up the stairs.

Finn opens the door for us with a silent nod. No one likes that we have to crack down on one of our own, especially not one in this position. His glowering expression, coupled with his stoic silence as we pass, shows he understands the situation more than Ms. O'Connor even does.

"End of the hallway on the left," I tell her. She walks on her own now, looking around at each open doorway as we pass. Ronan's woman, Maeve, sits on the sofa in the family room reading a book. She's at ease now after months of being in turmoil. At least the bloodstains have been washed off the walls now and the paint touched up.

Aisling's eyes track to the open door near the end of the hall. Ronan is waiting for us, but this won't be like other times. He won't go easy on her. She's really fucked things up again, and her carelessness may well start another war we'll have to fight. This one may prove to be worse than the last.

We round the corner into Ro's office. He's seated at his desk and looks up at us as we walk in. His eyes meet mine briefly, and I nod as he stands and gestures to the chairs across from his desk.

"Isla," he says smoothly, but the edge in his tone isn't easy to miss. It isn't easy to run a family the size of the O'Rourke Clan. Being chief fell on his shoulders after our father died, but Ronan proved himself our worthy leader when those less trusting of his skill rose up to prevent him from leading.

Aisling glares at him, but she sits where he indicated. Her lip is still twitching, but she's finally stopped wringing her hands. I stand behind her, watching down on her as Ronan sits back down. If this were any other person, any other crime, he'd have had her head already.

"So just say what you're gonna say and let me get back to work." She rolls her eyes, and Ronan's instant reaction is to clench his jaw.

"You can appreciate what sort of situation you've put me in, Isla." Ro drums his fingers on his desk. He's a man of few words, though at times, words have to suffice.

"Yeah? So..." She rolls her eyes. "It isn't like you've been a saint. Everyone in this city knows what you do. I just followed your lead." She crosses her arms over her chest, forcing her tits upward. I enjoy the bird's-eye view of her cleavage, which I don't even attempt to look away from. Every one of us O'Rourke men knows her position with us, and with Ronan bringing Maeve into his home, I'm pleased to know this beauty in front of me will wind up being mine.

It's not the way I thought I'd meet the woman I'd marry, but our father made an arrangement. We have to uphold that.

Ronan sits forward, steepling his fingers in front of himself as he says, "Isla, the arrangement your father made with mine doesn't give you immunity to do whatever the fuck you want. You can't just steal from my enemies and think there won't be repercussions." His dark glare is fixed on her as she squirms in her seat. If I could see her lip, I know I'd see it twitching.

"I didn't steal from you. Why the fuck do you care?" She's feisty. I like a challenge. So does Ronan. He's not going to go so easy on her at all.

"I care because those enemies are now coming after me."

"Why you? I'm the one they want." Aisling glances up at me, then back to Ronan. "You're not going to let them come after me, are you?" Her pale skin seems to blanch further. It scares her to think Eamon's men might hunt her down.

"We have an agreement with your family, Isla." Ronan sits back in his expensive leather Italian chair and runs a hand down his face. "I'm sending men to protect your family, but the damage is done. We need what you stole. It may be the only way to keep them off your back, and ours."

I don't know how much she stole, but the men who organized against Ronan in the wake of our father's death aren't jokers. Our cousin

Eamon had a gun to Ronan's head at one point. They don't mess around. Even if she only took a thousand dollars, she has to pay. There are very few ways to protect her from her inevitable death or dismemberment.

"I don't know what you're talking about—"

"Cut the shit!" he shouts, standing up so quickly that his chair falls over. He slams a hand down on his desk, and she jumps.

"I don't have it. I spent it." Aisling trembles. She knows how this works. It isn't the first time her family has had a run-in with ours. The name O'Rourke in Dublin is synonymous with power and influence—and death.

Ronan's eyes trace up to my face. "Did you find anything?" he asks, glaring at me.

"Nothing," I tell him. A search of her office and home revealed nothing. No money, no secret stash anywhere. It's possible it's hidden elsewhere, but I don't know where.

"Ms. O'Connor, if you can't return their money, they'll want you to pay in your blood. It's blood the O'Rourke Clan will not allow to be shed, so now you have to remain under our protection." Ronan now leans over his desk, palms splayed on the hard wood. His tie dangles under his body as he stares menacingly.

"Just let them take me." It seems like Aisling isn't afraid of the consequences of her actions. It's stupid and brazen.

"It's not that easy, and you know it." He pushes upward and straightens, then tucks his tie against his body and buttons his coat. His eyes lock on my face. "If she's hacked into their accounts, they'll potentially have a trace back to ours. Get Chester on that. Clean it up. We can't let our assets be exposed or made vulnerable." Then he looks down at her. "You really fucked up."

Aisling looks away from him. I have a mind to grab her head and force her to look back at him, but we promised her father that not a hair on her head would be harmed.

"Like I said, let them take me." She crosses her arms over her chest, and her shoulders seem to deflate a little, slumping slightly.

"You're bound to an agreement." Ro's gaze hardens on her. "You don't get a choice, Isla, and inciting anger in our enemies won't help you get out of it. You'll marry into this family by month's end." Ronan jerks his chin upward at me. "Take her to your house. She goes nowhere and does nothing until the wedding. It's the only way."

"Uh!" She scoffs, standing up. "You can't do that!"

Before she can dart out the door, my arm is around her waist, pulling her back. "Don't make this harder than it has to be, Isla," Ronan grumbles. "Declan, I'm trusting you. Don't fuck this up. You know what's at stake."

I nod at him as I wrestle the very angry woman in my arms. I do know what's at stake. I have to clear my name in my brother's eyes and make sure he understands that I'm on his side, and I'm going to do whatever it takes to redeem myself.

2

ISLA

"Get your fucking hands off me!" My shouting doesn't seem to faze Declan O'Rourke, nor does the way I pound my fists into his arm and side. I'm furious, ready to run as soon as he sets me down, but he's so strong even if I tried, I can't fight him. And with my luck, he'd run faster than me too.

"Feckin' woman, stop hitting me." Declan manhandles me through the door to his home, then up the winding staircase. I've not been here before. It's a large home with expensive marble flooring, large paintings on the walls, and old woodwork that seems original to the house.

All the O'Rourkes live like this, displaying their wealth like a badge of pride. Ronan's place was even nicer, though I didn't really take time to sit and admire the decorations when I was afraid of what he'd say. Somehow, this seems worse than any punishment he could've dealt out. I wanted a punishment. I wanted him to just smack me or tell me to pay him back for the trouble. This is way worse.

"I can fucking walk on my own." I continue to fight him on the climb up the stairs. My kicking and lashing out are my attempts to free myself, but it's exhausting me too. I kick over a table inadvertently, sending an expensive-looking vase crashing to the floor in a dozen pieces. Declan doesn't bat an eyelash. He stalks forward down the hall.

When he finally sets me down inside a bedroom, I shove him hard, then fix my suit jacket and slacks. "This is ridiculous!" I spit. My slacks are riding up, my hair frazzled. I run a hand over it to smooth it down, but nothing can smooth away my anger. "I want to go home."

"It's not safe," Declan grumbles. He shuts the door behind himself quietly then turns to let his eyes drink me in. I'm not immune to the effect of a handsome man in my presence admiring my good looks, but under these circumstances, I'm not thrilled with it.

"What do you mean, not safe? I live there. It's where all my belongings are." I'm heaving for breath after the wrestling match I just had. It was like banging against a brick wall.

"I mean it's gone, Aisling. They burnt it to the ground already. Do you understand? You're fucking with Ronan's biggest enemy right now, and they're not happy." He doesn't seem too pleased with me, either. He scowls at me and scratches his beard as his eyes study me.

He's probably the most handsome of all the O'Rourke men. I've always found myself attracted to his good looks and strength. I'd have told my sister only a few weeks ago that if this stupid arrangement went through and I couldn't escape like I hoped, Declan would be the one I'd want to marry most. Of course, based solely on looks. I hate the entire idea of arranged marriages, and marrying into this family sickens me. I want to get away from this. It's the only reason I've been skimming money from the O'Reilly Clan to begin with.

"How much?" Declan barks at me, and I turn away, walking toward a window on the far side of the room.

"The O'Reillys don't need the money anyway." I stop by the window and pull aside the thick black drapes. The room is gloomy, dark colors and low light—not at all like my brightly colored home which apparently is up in smoke now. I know my theft was risky, but far less risky than stealing straight from the O'Rourkes. That would've been a death sentence for me and my father. I just never thought the O'Reillys would notice so quickly. I hoped to be long gone before anyone caught on.

"How fucking much?" he demands very loudly. I edge the curtain back farther and stare out at the gloomy sky over Dublin. It's been raining for a few days now, matching my mood. This wedding gets closer every day, and my chance of getting to that cache in my father's back yard seems less and less likely.

"More than two hundred thousand," I tell him, turning to look him in the eye.

He steels his gaze, which he thinks is intimidating to me, but I've seen worse. Besides, how can you be intimidating when you're so spectacularly attractive? I'm supposed to be scared of those dark emerald eyes and such a manicured beard? He looks like he stepped off a cover of *Gentleman's Quarterly*. Doesn't even make me nervous, except for the flutter in my belly when he checks me out.

"What the hell were you thinking, woman?" He rakes a hand through his hair and loosens his collar by unbuttoning the top button.

"Risk over reward," I say dryly, turning back to the window. "I wanted out."

I catch a glimpse of a fleeting compassionate expression on his face as he moves toward me. Declan has an imposing presence, I'll give him that. He's a very large man with broad shoulders, thick biceps. I may have undressed him with my eyes a time or two. It makes my body hitch up a degree or two as he closes the gap between us.

"It's not all it's cracked up to be, Aisling. Getting out is dangerous. You're better off here."

"My name is Isla," I spit. "Fucking use it." I've heard it all before, Dad's lectures, Ronan's warnings, my mother's pleading. But none of them are a pawn in someone else's game. None of them have to walk down an aisle to marry someone they don't love just to pay back someone else's debt.

"Isla, I apologize." Declan's smooth-as-butter baritone makes me shudder. These men are animals, not to be trusted, not to be weak around. Hearing him speak like this only feels like a manipulation attempt. He's not sorry. He's loyal—to Ronan O'Rourke.

"Are you, then?" I move away from the window and him. I can't stand the smell of him—musky and intoxicating. It makes my body want to react to his nearness, the cologne that smells like pheromones intended to turn me on. If I stay next to him, I'll betray myself. As much as I am drawn to everything that is Declan O'Rourke, it's a matter of principle. Women are not pawns. I want to show my father respect, but I hate what he's done to me. The position he put me in.

"Isla, you don't seem to understand what you've done." He turns, his eyes following me across the room as I throw back the covers on the bed and toss pillows to the floor. I may as well get comfortable. I'm not going anywhere with him looming over me.

"No, I do. I've put together a plan to get the fuck away from you before you monsters force me to do something I never want to do." I'm not a fool. The inevitable looms in front of me, beckoning me closer while I try to find any escape route.

"You're walking down that aisle whether you like it or not. Your father made his debts. I'm afraid you don't get a choice. All you've done is make it more dangerous for yourself. Can't you see that?" He follows me, picking up the pillows I've thrown down and tossing them back to the bed. "The sooner you accept your fate, the sooner you'll be safe. No one wants to force you, Isla. This is about respect and honor."

"This," I spit, reeling around on him, "is about control. Which you seem to lord over me." I reach out to push him away, and he catches my wrist, glaring at me. His face is inches from mine. I watch his eyes drop to my lips, and I swallow against the lump in my throat as my pulse picks up. Being close to this man does things to my body that I hate. My temperature leaps up a thousand degrees as I pry my hand away from him.

"No one is trying to control you, woman. We're trying to keep your father's integrity and follow our father's orders. And we're trying to keep you safe." There's something there in his eyes—something he's not telling me. There's always something no one is telling me.

"I don't want your protection. I want freedom." My shoulders square. My eyes lock on his. My expression dares him to lay a hand on me, but he takes a step backward.

"You'll be my wife, and you'll be free, Isla. Just let me protect you." Declan backs away and walks toward the door. I say nothing as he slips out into the hallway and shuts the door behind himself.

For a split second, I think of running out, of getting past him and out the front door, but where would I even go? If I go to my father's house, they'll track me there faster than I could get to my cache and get my family to safety. When the door locks, I know I'm stuck here for the time being. They can't force me to stay forever. At some point, they'll look away for a second, and when they do, I'll be ready to move quickly.

I strip off my jacket and shoes and climb onto the bed. I've nothing else to wear, and I'm not partial to grown men walking in on me when I'm stripped down to my skivvies, so I curl up on the bed in my slacks and blouse and wait. All the rage coursing through my body will do me no good. What I need is calm, rational thought.

I want to scream and rage, pound on the door, demand to speak to my father, but I know how they control him too. The pressure they put on him would have him coaching me to just do as I'm told. I don't know what specific debt he has to pay back to them, but whatever it is requires my cooperation. It's required my cooperation for years now. Otherwise, I'd have never become their accountant. Now I know way too much for my own good.

If I try running, I have to do it right the first time and make sure I vanish. If not, I won't just have to hide from the O'Rourkes. I'd have to hide from his enemies and the Garda too. Everyone will want a piece of me when I'm out, and I have friends lined up to help me truly disappear.

I just have to get to the stash buried in my father's yard and safely to the port.

And I need to do it before they make me walk down that aisle.

3

DECLAN

So many memories filter into my mind as Ronan's car pulls up in front of the pub. It doesn't sit well with me, the newness of it all. I wait until the car stops before I open the door and step out. I can almost smell the ash in the air, though it's been months. My cousin died in the fire that destroyed the old pub. It was a real wakeup call for me at the time, a lesson I needed to learn before I made a huge mistake—a mistake I'm still trying to redeem myself from.

"So different," I mumble as Ronan steps out of his car and nods at his driver.

"New beginnings," he says curtly, though it doesn't feel like a new beginning.

Not so long ago, we were meeting a family member here for a similar reason. Eamon wanted control and fought us to his death. We only just buried him and his successor has a new reason to hate us. We've not met the man behind the mask yet, but he'll be here soon, the one pulling all the strings and who incited our cousin to turn against us.

"Still," I breathe. Burying so many family members in the past six months has challenged us all. We all need things to calm down so we can get our bearings. What Isla has done has only fanned flames to life again where we thought only ash and smoke remained, like the long-gone but not forgotten remnants of our family's meeting place. "Benny would have loved it."

Ronan nods at me, and we move toward the building. Lochlan watches over Isla for me, making sure our enemies don't find her location. For now, she's safe there, hidden within my walls awaiting the nuptials, which Ronan says should be very public. If I can convince her to walk the aisle willingly, it will be a miracle. She doesn't even realize the behind-the-scenes risks we're taking for her.

"Will he show?" I ask Ronan. We've heard his name is O'Reilly, but which of them, we're not sure. Three brothers got into Eamon's head and tried to divide us.

"Oh, he'll show. He has to. Imagine having hundreds of thousands of dollars stolen by a woman. The man's ego alone will be too large for the doorway." Ronan scrubs his hand through his hair and pulls open the door to the pub. I follow him in and breathe in the scents of whiskey and sweat. It's bittersweet seeing the brand-new dining room and knowing things in this family have been shattered so desperately, it will never be the same. But we're building toward a new normal. If we can get past this hiccup.

Ro and I each get a drink and take a seat. A few men mill around the place talking. Two stand in the corner playing darts. They're all part of the clan or know someone who is. We don't get many strangers here, and if they wander in, we help them find their way out. This is our sanctuary, a place we conduct business and relax. Today, it's the former, and I'm not pleased about it.

"He's going to make threats, Ro."

"Let him. We aren't the ones who took his money." Ronan nurses his whiskey with alert eyes scanning the room constantly.

"But we're harboring the woman who did," I point out, having a sip of my own drink. To him, this is cut and dry. He hopes to throw his weight around and scare them off, but if they're coming back so quickly after we took out their leader, this isn't going to go as well as my older brother thinks.

"And soon, she'll be an O'Rourke wife and he'll have to back off." Ronan's coolness is partly due to the fact that he has zero fears. The only time I've ever seen him ruffled was when someone threatened his partner. But some of it is because he's completely convinced that the old ways of doing things are still fully upheld in this world, which for the most part, they are.

But men like my late cousin don't always respect the rules, written or unwritten. We fought hard to protect Maeve from Eamon's antics, and now we might have the same fight on our hands for Isla. We've never had a woman in this world be a player in the game. Isla stole from them.

The door swings open and three men in dark suits enter. Their burly beards and dark swathes of hair give them away. They're not our family. And they're not the man we're waiting for, either. But they are here with him.

Sebastian O'Reilly follows them through the door. He undoes his suit jacket and loosens his tie as he nods at us and approaches where we sit. I can tell by the scowl on his face and how he flicks his hand, dismissing his men, that he's angry. Though, we knew he would be when we arranged this meeting. He walks with a chip on his shoulder, gripping his belt buckle as if he intimidates us.

Ronan doesn't even stand or raise a hand to shake his. With stern eyes, he watches Sebastian sit across from us and cross one leg over his other. No one says anything at first. It's the unspoken communication that we wait for—Sebastian's deepening scowl, the way he pulls his weapon out and releases the clip, then clears the chamber and lays it on the table. It's his sign that he's not here for violence—this time.

"I'm angry, Ronan." Sebastian is the first to speak, not mincing words.

"And?" Ronan sits straighter as he sets his tumbler on the table. My brother doesn't handle anything the way I would, but I'm here to observe and absorb. I have to read this man, learn his personality type, know what he might be thinking ahead of time. It's my job. If I'm going to enforce the arrangement we have with Isla's father and protect her at the same time, I have to know what I'm up against.

"And you understand what this means. Hand over the girl to me and we'll call it a day. She stole from me. I don't take that lightly." Sebastian's arm drapes over the table, fingers tapping on the wood surface next to where his weapon lies. His men hover just out of earshot behind him.

He sits coolly, not overly stiff or aggressive. His posture is laid back, but he isn't letting his guard down either. His hand so near his weapon is a warning to us that he's not afraid to use it if he needs to. Sebastian O'Reilly had no qualms about goading our cousin to attack us. There's no telling what he's capable of now that he's in charge.

"You're not getting the girl, Sebastian." I lean forward as I speak. I don't need Ronan's approval to do my job, which is protecting her. She'll be my wife, and I'm taking the stance right now that no man will lay a finger on her. Ever.

Sebastian's eyes track to mine. They're cold and hollow, the type of evil reserved for the devil. I've looked into eyes like his and seen the vile things men do in this world. There is no doubt in my mind that if this man got ahold of Isla, he'd kill her without remorse. Which makes me want to stand between him and her even more.

"You know the price she has to pay, O'Rourke. It's an honor thing." He nudges his gun clip with his finger and it spins in a circle. "I'd hate to have to get your family tangled up in this. Her father too... It would be a shame." He looks down for a second, and when he looks back up, his pupils seem to take over the whites of his eyes, making him look even more evil.

"You heard my brother. She's off limits." Ronan backs me up with the escalation of standing and buttoning his coat. I follow his movements, standing shoulder to shoulder with him. Most men tremble before even one of the O'Rourke men, and two of us make all men cower.

But Sebastian returns the free round to his clip, then slips it back into the magazine of his weapon and clicks it into place by slamming it on the heel of his hand before holstering it on his chest under his coat and standing up.

"You don't seem to understand. I will have what I want. She will pay for what she's done to me." He narrows his eyes on Ronan and then looks me up and down.

"She'll be my wife," I say with authority. "And if you lay a finger on her, your blood will join Eamon's in watering the earth." I wrap one hand around the opposite wrist and stand with my shoulders squared, staring into the beady eyes of my newest mortal enemy. The list is short, but this man made it.

He shakes his head, making his loose blond hair tousle around his face. "You're a funny man, Declan. Don't let anyone tell you otherwise." Sebastian extends a hand, which I stare at coldly. I'm not touching the fucker.

But Ronan takes his hand and shakes it. "Stay away from my family and we won't have an issue." Ronan's threat is backed by five brothers and more than a dozen cousins who will all—along with dozens of other loyal men—fight to protect Isla and any other woman Sebastian thinks he owns.

"I will get that woman," Sebastian says, gloating. "And when I do, she will receive just punishment for humiliating me and stealing from my family. And I'm not sorry for the collateral damage since you all seem foolish enough to run into battle for a wench like that." He withdraws his hand and nods at us. "Good day, then. And good luck."

Sebastian heads for the door, and his men follow him out in the same single-file way they came in. Ronan stands watching after him with his jaw tight and his eyes narrowed. I wait until they're gone and wonder what's going through my brother's head. He can't possibly want to go to war with this idiot over Isla regardless of any promise made to her father from ours.

"Go to her. Don't let her out of your sight. Make sure no one learns where she is, and for fuck's sake, get the wedding plans finished. She'll be safer when she carries our name." Ronan doesn't move, but I do. Swiftly.

"Got it," I tell him. I know what I have to do, which might be harder than I want it to be. Isla has a stubborn streak in her, and she won't take marrying me easily. I'm not happy coercing her, but if it's what I have to do to save her life, I will.

I walk out the door and see Sebastian's car's taillights as he pulls out of the parking lot while I walk to my car. He isn't going to get a chance to lay a finger on her because I'm going to protect her with my life. She reminds me of myself at that age. Twenty-two is so young and naive. She doesn't understand the dangers of this world. Neither did I. I wanted out at one point, and I almost made it out.

Then I realized what this family could do for me, how I was better off here. I have to show Isla that this is the best thing for her, to marry me and let me protect her. If not, she'll die and there will be nothing anyone can do to stop it.

4

ISLA

A few birds fly past the window as I pace, staring out at the cerulean sky. Three days they've kept me here under lock and key. Three days without contact with my family, without working, without seeing the sky except from behind the glass of this window. If I didn't know they'd come running and potentially harm me for doing it, I'd break the window and be gone.

But Declan and his brothers would know exactly where to find me. They may even be there before I get there. I want out of this house, out of this situation, but I have to plan carefully, think carefully. The O'Rourkes aren't wrong. Sebastian O'Reilly's men will kill me for what I've done because I was stupid enough to get caught.

Seeing the world moving on while I remain trapped, it's like those birds are mocking me. Time is marching onward for everyone and everything, and I'm stuck, frozen here behind these thick walls, awaiting my fate. Whether it's death, marriage, or a life on the run, there is a one hundred percent certainty that it involves suffering of some sort. My jaded heart knows that all too well.

I turn, peeling myself away from the window, and walk to the small wooden armchair in the room near the reading desk. The old roll-top smells musky, like it was stored in a place that allowed moisture to seep into the wood and begin to rot it. And the chair's green leather cushion has seen better days. I lower myself onto the seat and stare down at a book lying on the desktop.

I've been passing my time with a little reading. Today it's Dostoyevsky's *Crime and Punishment*. It fascinates me how the master weaved these words together to tell the tale of one's descent into madness, how easily the human mind can fall. I wonder, as I fold open the worn cover and lay the book flat before me, if that's what's going on with these O'Rourke men—the O'Reillys too. Are they gone mad with the sins they're committing? Is that why they hunger and thirst for death at every turn? Why their greed and lust run out of control? Why they think controlling people—controlling me—is a good thing?

My eyes pore over the pages, licking up every last word. The story is captivating, holding my attention, keeping me poised for whatever may come next. I sit like this for hours, devouring the characters and scenes, feeling pinned to the edge of my seat, anxious to turn the page, terrified of what it's uncovering in my own heart as I compare myself to Raskolnikov. Perhaps I am the mad one, not fighting back like I could, not running for the Garda's protection...

I'm there, hunched over the desk with the light creating a halo around me, hours later when Declan comes to the door. I hear the key and the lock, but the characters seem more real than my reality. At least, I'd like them to be. Being a fly on the wall watching a man grow less sane by the minute seems like a far better way to spend my time than locked away in a monster's home with a marriage I didn't ask for as my only exit.

"Dinner," he grunts gruffly, but I don't look up. I hear the clatter of dishes, liquid being poured into a glass, more dishes clattering. He belches. That's what gets my attention. I glance up to see him seated at the small table in the corner of the room.

He's dressed in all black. Black jeans that stretch down to his black leather boots. Black T-shirt that stretches over his thick biceps, an inky black tattoo peeking out from the sleeve. His hair is loose, but he wears it brushed back away from his face, and his beard is perfectly trimmed, like every other time I've seen him. He's attractive. I can't help noticing. Any woman in this world would kill for the chance to bed him.

My eyes physically ache from reading, and though he's easy on them, I look away. "Not hungry," I tell him. I want to finish this chapter, find out what happens next. Raskolnikov is in his home, sweating, waiting.

"It's going cold," Declan barks. He thinks I'm the sort of woman who will jump at his command, but he doesn't know me. They may have authority to command other people, but that authority doesn't extend to me. So I sit and read, ignoring the clattering of dishes that crescendos the longer I sit.

The ruckus becomes so distracting, I can't focus on the words anymore. I make a mental note of what page number I'm on so I can return to reading when he's done throwing his tantrum, but I continue to turn the pages and let my eyes roll over them. I won't give him the satisfaction of knowing he's been successful at pulling me out of my secret world of escape.

"Eventually, you'll have to talk to me," he says, and I know he's right. For now, however, I continue my ruse. This book is invigorating and he is not. Though I feel the tug on my chest, the actual fucking desire to look at him and admire his beauty.

An image forms in my mind now—not Sonya or Dunya as they minister to the man in the pages in front of me, but Declan, shirtless, stalking toward me. I've only seen him shirtless once, more than a year ago. And more by accident than anything else. I walked in on something I wasn't supposed to see when I stopped by Ronan's home the day I accepted the job of being his accountant—which I only took as a means to siphon money from their accounts.

But they became suspicious, and I shifted my focus on Eamon at that point.

That day still rattles me, seeing Declan biting down on a wooden spoon while a woman sewed his back shut, some sort of injury, not a gunshot. It sliced right through the tattoo he has there—a large bird of prey, long talons, haunting eyes. He looked up at me then, devouring me as he grimaced and fought through the pain. Those same eyes are on me now. I can feel them.

"And you'll find it easier to walk down that aisle with me if you just come get to know me."

His words snap me out of my trance. Even the most exceptionally beautiful body can't hide the darkness in a man's soul. It finds a way to seep out and bubble to the surface, like air under a rock beneath the water. When something shifts it, the bubbles rise. It's there in his eyes, the way he wants to control me, the darkness, the vile thoughts.

"I'm not marrying you," I snip back at him, shutting the book and pushing it away. I am hungry, and I'm not going to starve myself just to avoid conversing with him. I'm not giving him that power over me. He's not worthy of that much.

"You are." His statement sounds final, a command. He thinks himself a god over my life. I think he's a boy, immature and mal-informed.

"And will you open my mouth and make the words 'I do' come out?" I scoff as I sit down, taking a cloth napkin provided for me and snapping it before I drape it over my knee. The food does look delicious—steak, broccoli, and a baked potato. I didn't realize the O'Rourke men eat American style food. I'd much prefer champ potatoes and whiskey cream sauce, but this looks appetizing too.

"I won't have to." His eyes flick up at me as he takes another bite. Then he chews carefully as he watches me. There is a storm in them, a tempest ready to unleash its fury on an angry emerald sea. I have to look away. His gaze warms my body to a balmy temperature that has me sweating. Or maybe it's the heat on this steak.

"You're confident for a man who knows so little about women. Don't you realize I need clothing? Toiletries? A shower now and then?" The bath is there, an old claw-foot antique he's had restored to the original sheen of a polished enameled cast-iron. The gilded feet would fetch him thousands each, but to an O'Rourke, money is nothing. They probably use it to stoke fires in the winter. That's what made skimming off the top so easy for so long. They don't even miss it.

"I can arrange anything you want, Aisling. I'm not your enemy. I'm here to protect you." His edge softens, curls around me, sucking me closer, coaxing my body to warm further.

"I told you, my name is Isla." No one calls me Aisling besides my mother, not even Da. "And I told you, I don't need your protection." My insides tremble a little as I say the words. I know I can't fight Sebastian's men on my own.

"I prefer Aisling." His fork drops to his plate, his hand to his lap. He brings his napkin to his mouth to wipe, then discards it on the table next to his plate.

"I don't," I snip, now feeling flustered by this ogre. He's staring at me, unnerving me with his eyes again, probably undressing me. The way I was undressing him in my mind moments ago. We have chemistry. It makes my body flush. Warmth pools in my core as arousal heightens every sense.

The dynamic of power he has over me is both electrifying and suffocating. I want to lean into it and feel the exhilaration of attraction, let my heart race and my body get out of control with desire. But I also want to fight it, push back against nature and my physiological response to his nearness, and put him in his place.

"You do need my protection, though." He stands and stares down at me, making the captor-captive dynamic stronger—my pulse too.

"Sebastian will kill you the first chance he gets, and he won't even make it quick. He'll likely cut your fingers off one by one, feed them to his dogs right in front of you, and then bleed you out, one drop at a time. And when he's done with you, your father will be next."

The sickening thought that my crime against that man may come back to harm my father makes my stomach roll. I'm not hungry anymore. Not even close. And the arousal that was just so gloriously warming my core cools. I shudder. I need his help because I can't fight my own battles, and I know Da can't either. How would an old man, almost sixty, fight a criminal organization?

"Fine," I grumble, but I don't mean it. I need him to believe I mean it. I need him to make sure he's watching over my father until I can get to my cache and safely get my family away from here.

"Fine?" he asks. His fingers trail over my shoulder, brushing a few strands of my dark hair behind my back. His touch is gentle, not at all what I expect from a man like him.

"Fine, I'll marry you. But you protect my family..." The words taste bitter on my tongue. It's a total lie, and it comes so easily. After months of skimming, I've become something I'm not. Something I hate. I've become one of them.

My eyes trace up his body, see the ridges on his chest beneath the thin T-shirt that hides his muscles. I think he wears it too small on purpose. He's a large man. I admire what I can see and what I imagine too. But maybe it's his determination to protect me that does it.

"I've already got men at your father's home." He pats my shoulder and starts walking. "And we'll bring you anything you want—clothes, shoes... Feel free to enjoy a bath."

And just like that, he's gone and I'm hating myself again. I give in so fucking easily. All it took to make me putty in his hands was that? I'm shockingly weak, and my body needs to get in check or it's going to get me in trouble. The kind I can't get out of so easily.

5

DECLAN

No one has heard from Isla O'Connor in a few weeks. She's been locked away at my home while hers was burned to the ground. The news broadcasts report her as missing, and the ongoing investigation isn't ideal for Ronan, considering Isla is his accountant, but Sebastian's men destroyed any shred of evidence when they set that fire. It's the saving grace I ponder while Nicholas drives Brynn and me toward her father's home.

"Ya think he's gonna cause a problem?" Brynn, my second cousin and the troublemaking type, studies his weapon, which he holds in his hand rather than having it holstered like mine.

He's young and green, at least when it comes to this sort of business. I'm an enforcer, not a killer. There's no need for a weapon today. Mick O'Connor is well aware of the arrangement we have with him. It was his idea, a means to an end.

"Put that thing away." My eyes flick to the window as we pass fields of barley, large, sweeping meadows where cattle and horses graze. "O'Connor isn't an enemy." I'm enforcing the arrangement, and I'm doing O'Connor a favor at that. His daughter would be dead already without Ronan's quick thinking and my action.

I feel the heat radiating off Brynn. He's here for action, to let some steam off. He doesn't understand the tact required in this position. I can feel his eyes burrowing into my skin as he stares at me, but I don't even dignify his gaze with a response. His demeanor is off, aggressive even toward me.

"You can't ever be overprepared." The grunt is his rebuttal, but he knows I'm in charge. He slides his weapon into a shoulder holster below his left arm, nestled under biceps so thick it's comical. The man has nothing better to do than sit in a gym for hours a day and body build. I'm fit. He's a meathead.

The car rumbles to a stop in the long, winding gravel drive just past the old towering barn to the right. A fence line runs the entire property, hedging in pastures and fields. The O'Connor family aren't farmers, but to every appearance, they seem to be. I push the door open and see one of the hired hands in the field next to a few cows—a ruse, covering the deeper operations here housed in other outbuildings.

"Mornin'," the man calls. "What can I do fer ye?"

"Mick?" I call out. Fog cloaks the old far property, holding the sun at bay this morning. Its thick moisture is heavy in the air, palpable as I shut the car door and hear Brynn shut his.

"In the house. Mind ye, the Missus weren't too keen on hearin' 'bout the fire." The man nods his head, and I watch a bulge in his lower lip shift as he spits into the alfalfa he stands on.

I tip my chin up and meet Brynn at the front of the car. We walk toward the house in silence. I imagine they're either devastated over the fear of losing Isla to our enemies or they've settled it that she died in the fire. I've no way of knowing what they're thinking. Ronan hasn't sent them word yet. That's my job today. For once, I get to bring good news to someone and not just lead and smoke.

"*Jaysus!*" Brynn grumbles as he shakes his head. "Doesn't even have the decency to come out when he sees us walking up." The dark expression he wears irritates me. His overinflated sense of ego makes me bristle. We do command respect, but this family is our ally.

I knock on the door and wait. There is shuffling there behind the door, and it swings open. Rebecca O'Connor, eighteen years old, not even finished with her schooling, stands with wide blue eyes and a pale complexion. Her strawberry hair is tangled, fuzzed around her face with curls springing outward. I can see she's been crying, as I expected they'd all been doing. She wipes her cheek and nods, stepping backward.

"Come in, Mr. O'Rourke..." There is a resignation in her tone, as if she's surrendering to fate. I wonder if Mick has told her about the arrangement with Isla and me. If they think Isla has passed on, whether they are already preparing Rebecca for her fate now. She's beautiful and any man would be lucky to have her, but her time hasn't come yet.

"Your father?" I ask. I notice her stiffening as Brynn's eyes sweep up and down her body. She's wearing pajamas, a long, thick nightgown that disguises her feminine form.

"Through the kitchen," she says, nodding, and I rest my hand on the butt of my weapon as I tilt my head in that direction, standing between Brynn and the pale beauty he seems enamored with.

"Thank you," I tell her, and she nods again.

When Brynn has moved on, I follow him. We move together past the living room and into the dining room. The kitchen hosts a table and chairs in the far end for breakfast and Old-World-style cabinetry on the far end. The modern appliances seem out of place, but in a three-hundred-year-old farmhouse, anything made of stainless steel would.

Mick stands behind Brennan, his beautiful wife, with his chin rested on her shoulder, his arms wrapped around her middle. They stare out the window over the sink as she holds a bowl in one hand, wash rag in the other. It appears she's cleaning up from breakfast, and though there are tears streaming down her cheeks, she is every bit as beautiful as Isla. I can see where the younger girl got her good looks.

Mick looks up at me, straightening and squaring his shoulders. I've been here dozens of times. In my position, I see a lot of Mick and a lot of other men who work with us. Mick's tired eyes train on me for a moment, then sweep to take in Brynn. They've never met, but I can see the recognition in Mick's eyes. He knows we're here about his daughter.

"Do we have to do this here?" he asks. His hand still rests protectively on Brennan's side. She glances up at me. Her normal, cheery disposition has been replaced with that of a grieving mother. The whole atmosphere of this house is heavy.

"She's not dead, Mick." My words carry authority on every occasion, but in this instance, it makes them both stand taller and pay attention. "Just the house was lost. She's with me, at my home."

I fold my hands together in front of myself and rest my arms against my body as I sigh. The words sink in slowly, but Brennan begins to cry and clings to Mick. He embraces her, and any trace of mourning flashes away instantly. There is anger in his eyes, probably a demand for vengeance and justice. I cool him with another comment.

"And no, we didn't set the fire." My tongue draws over my lower lip. It's time to call in his debt, and the slight nod he gives me in response tells me he understands. I don't have to do much enforcing on this. He's more than eager to make this transaction with me. If anyone understands the stakes, it's him. "Did you know she was skimming?"

I feel Brynn beside me growing antsy. I'm sure he'd rather be throwing fists, pounding Mick's face. I prefer to keep violence to a minimum unless absolutely necessary. There is no need to be pushy here.

"Skimming? Declan, you know I'd never permit that. Isla is a good girl. I'm sure she—"

"It wasn't from us, you langer." Brynn takes a step toward him, fingers balled into fists. "Now tell us what you know."

Mick's eyes flick from Brynn to me and back. He's nervous and flighty. "She's a good girl, Declan," he repeats. "She would never…"

"She did, and a lot." My calmer tone seems to ease him. He steps backward and holds Brennan closer. "She's not harmed, but if the men she stole from find her, she will be. It's time to enact the plan. It's the only way to protect her, and you, now."

Brennan's head rises and she shakes it. "You can't. She has years left. She's not ready. Please." For a woman who just found out her once-thought-dead daughter was alive, she should be happier to know that the worst to happen to her would be marriage.

"Oh, go have a whinge outside, ya banshee." Brynn jerks his chin upward and walks toward them, pushing her away as he grabs Mick by the front of his shirt. "Ya knew about the skimming, din't ya?" Brynn's aggression is completely out of line. These people won't fight me more than just a bit of complaining, and we have business with them. To upset the entire O'Connor family would be to start yet another war. The man has no tact at all.

"Declan?" Mick's frustrated eyes turn toward me. He won't fight back against Brynn at all. He knows what that would mean, but I can see how this is pushing the boundary of our agreement.

"Step off, Brynn…" I glare at him as he glances at me.

"The Muppet knows somethin' and we need to bring it back to Ro." Brynn's gaze hardens, and he throws a fist into Mick's gut.

I charge forward as Mick doubles over and exhales in a grunt. Brennan gasps and shrieks. She starts crying harder and cowers in the corner by the sink, covering her mouth. I grab Brynn's wrist and wrest him away from Mick before he can strike again.

"Wait in the car," I order, and he yanks his arm from my grasp. The heat of my gaze scorches him, making him loosen the collar of his button-down as he takes a few steps backward. My word is final and he knows it.

Brynn steps out, and I help Mick to a chair where he sits down. As we move, I see Rebecca standing in the far corner of the room, where the hallway to the bedrooms meets the small breakfast nook in darkness. Her eyes are wide with fright, her hand fluttering around her neck. Neither of these women got their emotional reactions from their mother. She's still bawling, now drawing a glass of water for her husband.

"Mick, I'm just here to pass it on. Sebastian O'Reilly is out for blood. I've had my men keeping tabs on your property, but that'll increase now. He wants her dead, and you after that." I stand with my hand on his shoulder as his head bobs.

"And the wedding then?" Mick's question makes Brennan whimper and cry louder. It's unpleasant for her to see her eldest daughter married off to align our families, but Mick made his bed and now he has to lie in it.

"Two weeks, maybe three. As quickly as we can arrange it... You know how this works. If she bears my name, it's safer." The unwritten rule that wives of made men mustn't be touched still stands. Isla O'Rourke means something different from Isla O'Connor. Even Sebastian O'Reilly will know that.

Mick sighs and sips the water as his head continues to bob. He looks up at Rebecca, whose eyes aren't quite as wide now. "I assume it's you, then?" Mick asks as his gaze sweeps up to mine. Ronan made the choice of which O'Rourke brother would marry her. I'm just the one he chose. I nod. "Then take good care of her. Let us know when and where we have to be for the ceremony..." He pauses for a moment and says, "Does she need anything?"

"I can take care of her needs," I say, but I turn to Rebecca. "But she will need some clothing. Everything she had was burned in the fire." Rebecca nods obediently and scurries away. This whole family is terrified of me because of my name, but one day, I'll show them that I am just the son-in-law, nothing to be scared of.

I wait for Rebecca to bring a bag of clothes, finish up a few business-related things with Mick, and then meet Brynn near the car. He's using the cuff of his suit jacket to polish the steel of his gun. He doesn't even look up when I approach. The tough-guy act is bullshit, something I won't tolerate. I'm ready to give him a tongue lashing when he speaks up.

"Everyone knows you almost defected, Declan." His almost-black, beady eyes unnerve me. There is a sinister energy to him, one I felt oozing off Eamon, my dead cousin, every time we spoke. "You're a traitor, and the only reason you still have breath is because our leader is your brother. But you're not fooling the rest of the family. I'll have your position when Ronan sees you for what you really are."

My anger gets the better of me and I dish out a little of the rage Brynn took out on Mick a few moments ago. My fist slams into his gut, doubling him over, and I spit on the ground near his feet.

"You follow my orders. If you ever do something like that again without my specifically telling you to, you'll have a hole between your eyes and your mother will be crying over a coffin."

So that's what his problem is? He thinks he knows me better than Ronan. This man has a lot to learn. He'll never become an enforcer as long as I'm living, and I'm a faster draw. He's going to learn his place in the food chain the hard way, and I'm going to be the one to teach him.

6

ISLA

If it isn't bad enough that I have to marry the dolt, he's sent in a fancy wedding seamstress. I don't get to pick my dress or even the material. She's chosen something really scratchy and uncomfortable. The pins she is using to adjust the bodice to make alterations stick into my skin every so often, prompting a wince and a yelp. Like now as she works on the right side under my arm.

"Do you have to be so damn rough?" I snap. The strapless bra Rebecca sent to me is stained by my blood now, but there's nothing to be done about it. The woman working on this dress is either shaking in fear of my attitude or she's inept and shouldn't be sewing.

My eyes shift to the full-length mirror Declan had brought in when he asked what I wanted. I got the bag of clothes from my sister, but there were simple things I missed. This mirror is one of them. My reflection reveals my own emotion, disgust, anger, probably fear if I look at myself long enough.

"Sorry, mum," the woman mutters for the fiftieth time. "I've no idea why my hands er shakin' so bad." Her head dips, and she sighs as she pulls the thick material away from my body. It can't be easy for her coming into an O'Rourke home and working like this. I wonder if she's here under duress, if I should be kinder.

My own mum often had women come in to make clothing for us, but farm life is slower than the chaos of organized crime—the pace set for darkness. We're kinder people too, more generous. Ronan O'Rourke and all four of his brothers are monsters who hold my father hostage to their deceit. It's why I need to get away from them, need to get my father away.

"I'm sorry too," I tell her softly, remembering who I really am. Working for them for so long has made me jaded and angry. It's not who I am. I'm just a woman who got caught up in the wrong mess. I can't even blame my father. He had his debts, true, and he could've found a different way to pay them off. Something tells me the O'Rourkes just twisted the knife and he had no way to back out.

The seamstress's eyes flick up to mine and she nods, but there is still fear there. I want to put her at ease, tell her I'm not a monster, not one of them, but the door swings open. My attention moves to the motion and I watch Declan stroll in. He's dressed in a dapper fashion, fitted charcoal suit, long black tie. His beard is trimmed neatly again, charged emeralds poring over my body.

"It's beautiful. Thank you, Raina." His words set into motion some strange reaction in the seamstress. I feel her hands on my back, then the zipper being pulled down. Suddenly, I'm standing naked, the dress pulled downward over my body as she forces me to step out of it.

My cheeks feel hot and my body flushes. The woman scurries away with the gown and her pincushion still wrapped to her arm. Her nervous skittering topples the bedside table, makes the candle on the other one jostle, and then she's gone, leaving me standing in just my bra and panties in front of the man whose eyes devour me.

"Beautiful," he says again, unbuttoning his suit coat. I stand tall, but my body wants to fold in on itself. The way he drinks me in is erotic and sensual. I push it away, not wanting to be flustered like this. I like his attention a little more than I should. I always have. Like last night when I dreamed he was on top of me, pleasuring me. Those things my mind concocts while I'm sleeping aren't in my control, are they?

"What do you want?" I snip, crossing my arms over my chest. This bra is a little on the small side, making my cleavage a bit too obvious, which I don't notice until the position of my arms makes it worse. Declan's eyes drop there, to the swell of my breasts.

"I came to discuss the wedding with you... I see the clothing Rebecca sent was acceptable." His eyes don't leave my chest as he prowls closer. Heat zings to my core at the way he's looking at me. How often does a young woman dream of a moment like this, where a man is captivated by her, riveted? My mind thinks horrible, nasty, dirty thoughts about him and what he could do to me.

"Are they safe?" I say, ignoring his comment. I have to do or say something to keep my mind off the fact that I'm extremely aroused by him. I turn away, staring at the book lying open on the roll-top. The seamstress interrupted me. I was almost finished with my latest obsession, *Gulliver's Travels*.

"Your family is protected." Declan stops in front of me and uses the back of his knuckles to brush up and down my cheek softly. The action sends more warmth pooling in my body. It's so gentle I can't hate him for it, but I do. I hate being any man's pawn, feeling his steely eyes rake across my bare flesh. I'm supposed to be cherished... That's what this touch says. But it's not what he's doing by forcing me to wed him. Not even close.

"You'll be protected too, Isla." His voice is low now, rumbling up from his belly and vibrating my chest. My heart wants to flip and jump up into my throat with rage, but my body wants him to continue touching. It elicits moisture between my thighs which I'm sure he can smell. I can.

"I told you, I don't need your protection." It's not hard to keep my tone hostile, not when I think of Rebecca and how innocent she is. With

THE ENFORCER'S REDEMPTION

men like this out there, and my father who has other "debts", I feel like I owe it to her to stop this, to get my entire family away from this world so she and I can both be safe.

"Oh, well maybe that's true..." His hand drops, finding a few strands of my dark hair and pushing them over my shoulder. Then his fingers trail down my arm and across to my wrist. A single thumb brushes across the lip of my strapless bra's cup, teasing my flesh. Goosebumps rise on my arms and thighs. I steel myself, not wanting to respond.

"Maybe it's you I need to be protected from?" My voice lilts as if it's a question, and the way he's making me feel, I can't hide the way my body is responding. My chest rises and falls faster than it should, betraying me. God, I want him to do unearthly things to me.

"A predator, is that what you think I am?" When he pinches my chin and forces me to look up at him, I see the desire in his eyes. No doubt if I reached to his groin, I'd find him hard as a rock. "Cheeky mare... Is this the way you're playing me? Hard to get? You want me to hunt you... I see how turned on you are. Your lips are blood red. They were the instant Raina took that dress off you and bared you for me. Your chest is a jackrabbit, Isla." The pad of his thumb pinches my skin to his finger and he smirks. "Oh, I'd hunt you."

"Stalk you across this room, pounce on you as if you were my kill, and then I'd spread you and devour you, drop by drop of that delicious moisture you make." His smirk intensifies and he chuckles. My body is rebelling against what I know is the right thing. My groin aches, my pussy pulsing. "Would you like that?"

"Get away from me," I hiss, but I don't mean it. He knows I don't. He's read me like one of my books, except my books are fiction, and this arousal is very real.

"Isla, stop fighting nature." The Declan who is gentle and calm with me returns. His breath dusts my face. Though I avert my eyes, I'm unable to turn my head. I watch in my periphery as he licks his lip and stares now at my mouth. My core is throbbing.

"I'm marrying you on a precept, not because I want you. And I'm doing it to save my father." The words come out choked, stiff. What I wouldn't give to feel the stubble of his beard scraping at my inner thighs right now. I have to get my body under control or I'm going to wind up fucking him and making this more complicated. The first chance I get to leave this place, I have to take it, and I don't want any regrets.

"I'm marrying you, and when I do, you'll be fully mine. Those tits, that hot body, your tight ass. And I'm going to show you how a real man treats a woman. You'll melt..." He's so close now, I think I can hear his heartbeat. My eyes can't turn away anymore. I'm almost whimpering in desire, and my insides feel like lava. "You belong to me," he says, and my hand flies before I even know what I'm doing.

The smack is loud and hard. It hurts my palm more than him. He doesn't even move. His posture doesn't shift. His hand remains on my chin just as gently. But he closes his eyes for a second. When he opens them, the beast is there.

"I belong to no one."

"We'll see," he grunts as he backs away. "But the only things I protect with my life are the things that I own." Declan buttons his jacket and turns. He calls over his shoulder, "The wedding is in two weeks, so settle in to that thought, Princess. And I promise to make the wedding night extra special."

I'm seething as he shuts the door behind himself. I pick up the book from the desk and throw it, not even caring that I've lost my page. Tears threaten to well up, but I refuse to be broken. I won't marry him. I won't be someone's pawn, no matter how badly my body wants his dick inside me. I will fight for myself and my sister, and I will win.

7

DECLAN

If my house is an estate, Ronan's is a palace. The gated property is hedged in by towering evergreens and a tall wrought-iron fence, making it the perfect venue for my nuptials with Isla. He wants complete control of everything, leaving no variables or chance of the event being interrupted. I agree.

"So we'll set up the marquee here. It's large. We're expecting a nice attendance." Ronan's arm rises in a sweeping gesture. His garden terrace is the perfect place for a wedding, larger than mine and shrouded in privacy thanks to the flora his gardener grows.

"But a tent? Ro, we're talking about one of the largest weddings of the decade." I'm skeptical about his plans, but a wedding this time of year, this close to the coast and outdoors, is sketchy. Using a large tent would give our guests shelter from the sun or rain, whatever the weather decides to do.

"You'll see." He grins at me like a fool. "Maeve has a whole team of planners working on this. Our business is safety." He nods curtly as he points to the far reaches of the garden near the back fence. "We need men stationed there and there." His finger points to the side. "We'll have the place surrounded and we'll have snipers on the roof—spotters if anyone asks."

It won't just be the O'Rourkes and the O'Connors here. There will be officials from the city and a few members of the Garda, not for show, either. They're loyal family friends, but they represent an important faction in this business. They keep the family straight and the laws and bylaws upheld. I want this to go exactly as planned.

"You really think Sebastian will care that Isla's last name will change? She stole from them." The significance isn't lost on me. In this world, it's not an eye for an eye. If so, returning the money would've been the first thing Ronan did.

"A man like Sebastian won't give a single fuck if her name changes." Ronan looks me in the eyes, and I see the way his brow furrows. The system was set up by old men centuries ago. They upheld the rules and traditions and so do we, but it doesn't mean Sebastian O'Reilly will. "But there will be hell to pay if he even thinks of touching her once she has your name. And how will he even get close to her if she's under your roof before then?"

Ronan makes a good point. Isla is safe as long as she's in my custody, but she's fighting me. I know that given the first chance, she'll run, and what then?

"And what will we do if he crosses that line?" My chest is tight, shoulders stiff. This isn't just about Isla becoming my wife. Of course she is a stunningly attractive woman, and the fascination I have for her makes it hard to use temperance when I'm around her. I thirst to have her. But that's not what this is about.

Isla O'Connor could die tomorrow and it would be a thorn in my shoe. I'd get over it, move on, find a different woman, one whom I would love. It wouldn't faze me much.

But the alliance her sacrifice—my sacrifice, if you call it that—is bringing both empowers and unites the O'Rourke family to a higher destiny, a divine purpose in this city. And I, for one, intend to make sure my father's wishes are upheld. Even if it means putting my life on the line. The only way Mick O'Connor sticks to his guns and does as he agreed to do is if Isla is safe.

"I'd like to think we'll cross that bridge when we come to it." Ronan purses his lips and stares off in the distance. It isn't easy leading the entire organization that has grown and multiplied over the years. I watched the strain it put on my father, thought of taking flight just the way Isla wants to. It's a lot for anyone to cope with, knowing what we do on a daily basis, how much darkness is in my lineage. Ronan carries it with grace, makes these decisions with wisdom and tact.

"But?" I prompt when he doesn't say anything.

"But Sebastian is two steps ahead of us. We can't let him get further ahead." He turns to me. "We have a plan to wed her to you and that should suffice, and should it fail, I have my own plan." I'm not sure if Ronan is talking about a different plan to finish what my father started by arranging this marriage or if it is a plan for vengeance against our enemies.

My plan is to fight like hell to protect my future wife and to continue that mission even long after she is in my bed and bearing me children. If O'Reilly comes after her then, he'll really see the devil rise. I'll bleed him dry and kill his entire organization one by one.

"Oh, there you are," Maeve calls, and I turn to see her beaming smile. Her hair is tied up into a bun and she wears a light yellow, cotton shift. The way Ro softens when he sees his own future wife reminds me that the harsh realities I'm facing don't have to be the only things in my life. I just have to convince Isla I'm not the monster she thinks I am. I didn't make this arrangement, and I'm a prisoner to it as much as she is.

"Maeve..." Ronan kisses her once then pulls her against his side. "We were just starting to discuss security."

"Oh, good." She smiles and turns to me. "Are you looking forward to this? I know it's so soon. You must be so in love." Maeve is naive, brought here by Ronan in her own little tangled web. She has no clue about the darker side of this family and the way we conduct our business. She only knows that Ronan is the head of the organization, and she chooses to remain blissfully unaware because she loves him.

"I'm eager to get this over with," I say, and while I mean it in the best possible way, she laughs, thinking it's a joke.

"Well, I can't wait. A wedding is such an exciting thing." Her hand smooths across Ronan's chest. I'm sure she's hoping for her own dream wedding and just practicing on mine to pass the time until Ronan decides the heat has died down enough that he has the capacity to have his wedding.

"Thank you for taking time to plan things and make it nice. Isla just isn't up for it." My gratitude toward my future sister-in-law is real, though the pretense would upset her if she knew why she was the one put in charge.

"Oh, I understand. The poor thing... She must be devastated about the house fire. You send her my well wishes and make sure she knows I'm here if she wants to talk." She looks up at Ronan and nuzzles his nose with hers. "Would you meet me inside soon? I have a few things to go over as far as the marquee goes. The company will have to set up, and I'd rather you be here when they come."

"Of course," he replies, kissing her again. It isn't hard to see how desperately my brother has fallen for her. I turn my eyes away as they kiss again and imagine Isla's lips on mine.

People think the arrangement of marriage is only something that the woman hates, but it's not true. Men want the woman of their dreams every bit as much as a woman wants her dream man. I'm just the lucky eejit who scored the only goddess in Dublin to be arranged to marry. She's perfect, while I'm scarred and hollow inside. I don't deserve this, or her. I want a chance to show her that she's incredible and I'm in awe—the way Ronan's eyes tell Maeve she's exquisite every time he looks at her.

"I'll see you later," Maeve tells me as she walks away, and when she's gone, I sigh and turn back to Ronan.

"Where were we?" he asks. "Right—security."

Ronan dives into the essentials, running everything past me. I don't really get a choice since it's his property and he's the head of this family, but I'm honored that he is going overboard to make sure this thing is a success. I'm not stupid enough to think it's personal, that he's doing it for me. I know he's doing this—beefing up security—because of the stakes. He has to follow through, and that means making sure this goes off without a hitch.

I listen to him and grunt in approval every so often, but my mind is stuck on Brynn now and how he reacted to me. I don't deserve Isla or this marriage. I don't deserve to be the one chosen for the honor of marrying her, aligning our family for greatness. I deserve the back of my brother's hand, or worse, the muzzle of his gun. Brynn was right. I almost betrayed my family.

Shame is the least of my worries. Guilt constricts my throat, weighs me down. To think I almost entertained my cousin Eamon's accusations against Ronan's character, almost walked away from my family. And Brynn knows it all. He can't tell Ronan anything he doesn't already know, but he can cast doubt on my current disposition and loyalty.

For a moment, I consider telling Ronan about it, about how Brynn is gunning for my position as enforcer. About how aggressive he was with Mick and what he said to me about the family's thoughts about me. This thing—marrying and protecting Isla—is my chance at redemption. It's my chance to show Ronan that I am loyal to this family. I'm not going to turn my back, and I never should have entertained the idea that Eamon presented to me.

"You okay?" he asks, and I realize I've not been listening to him.

"Fine... go on," I tell him with a nod, and he continues talking about where guards will be positioned and how many guns we'll have on the property.

Already, I sense something stirring, something sinister brewing in the atmosphere. I don't need Isla O'Connor in order to prove my worth, but I do need her. I need her to tether me to this Earth before my own desperation to run and find a new path forward kicks back in. I see it in her eyes, that desperation, the fear. I know because I've felt it. And while I'm not afraid anymore, I'm still desperate. I need to prove I'm something someone can rely on, and for some reason, I feel myself needing to prove it to her.

My phone buzzes and I pull it out of my pocket. Ronan stands patiently as I scowl at it and swipe to answer.

"Go," I say.

"Declan, there's an issue. You need to come back." Finn, my younger brother but not by much, has been watching Isla. I have no clue what's going on, but my gut tells me it's not good.

"I'll be there in fifteen minutes." Ronan is already moving away from me as I hang up the call. He is a man on a mission.

"I'll finish up. Go sort out your wife," he calls over his shoulder, and I scowl as I move toward the car. This had better be good or I'm going to be pissed.

8

ISLA

The sun is hot. I like it this way, when the sunlight warms my skin to the point I can feel the moisture drying out, stinging it. It's the first time in a week I've been allowed to go outdoors. Otherwise, I'd have been on this patio next to Declan's garden every day. Finn is nicer than his brother by far—or more naive. I can't tell.

"I'd like more lemonade, please," I tell his maid, and she nods at me and scurries off. I've had lunch, a bit of tuna salad with crackers and some lemonade. And I've been plotting my escape.

Only one guard stands over me, a man in his early fifties with greying sideburns and strong shoulders. He stares off into the distance not watching me, but he stands close enough to me that I could reach out and touch him if I wanted to.

"Lovely day, isn't it?" I ask him, toying with the idea of running from him. I don't know what lies on the other side of the tall pine trees near the back of the property, but I hope it's a pathway to freedom.

Dublin has so many neighborhoods, it'd be hard to tell where I'm even at to have someone pick me up. If I play my cards right, however, I could call Mum and Da and have them dig up the money I buried in their back yard without their knowledge. I could get them to meet me somewhere central and we could vanish together. It would be safer than my going to their house. Declan's brothers aren't likely to be following them, either.

"It's average," the guard says, tucking his thumbs into his belt. His biceps are as large as my thighs, tattoos snaking down both arms. He's scary and intimidating, but I know I could get his phone off him without his noticing it. It's clipped into a case that hangs from his belt, tempting me.

"Well, I think it's gorgeous. I'd love a walk around the property." A bird takes flight from the bush nearest the stone patio. The leaves shake, and the man's attention zones in on the movement as if preparing for danger. My hands think for themselves, reaching out and snatching the phone. Once I've got it, I don't know what to do with it. I bury it in my soft yellow skirt and tuck my head down for a moment. If it rings, I'll be caught.

"Just finish your lunch," he grumbles, and he looks down at me briefly before returning to stare out over the garden.

I swallow hard and glance up at him. He's not looking at me now, and I feel the tiny switch on the side of the phone with my fingernail and slide it to silent mode. Even a vibration at this proximity would be heard, but I have to risk it. I have to have a way to call my father and let him know I'm alright. If they've seen the fire at my home, surely, they'll assume the worst. I don't assume a man like Ronan O'Rourke knows anything about having compassion for a victim's family.

"I want a walk," I repeat, and this time, I don't take no for an answer. I rise slowly, wiping my face with the cloth napkin in a move that masks what my left hand is doing. The guard steps back, giving me more space, and I slide the phone into the waistband of the skirt and cover it with the flowing hem of the white blouse I'm wearing. "And I'm taking a walk."

My eyes meet his, and he scowls at me and rolls them, but he doesn't stop me when I start down the path. I hear his footfalls on the cobblestones behind me, almost like he's stalking me. I wonder if Declan ordered them not to touch me because if I had defied Ronan like this, certainly, his men would be all over me.

"The lupins are beautiful," I say absently, hoping to draw his attention to the flowers. The colorful spikes grow on either side of the path next to foxglove and lavender. The fragrant mixture perfumes the air, making me smile. If I didn't have such a hatred for the way I'm being forced against my will to marry a man I don't love, I'd admire the green thumb it took to grow these beauties.

"Bloody hell," he says, and I turn to see him patting his side.

"What is it?" I ask, and he glares at me.

"Don't go anywhere. I dropped my phone." The hulking man has his hand on the butt of his gun, and I wince as I realize I could've taken the weapon instead of the phone, but this is my opening.

"Of course, I'm just admiring the flowers." My hand caresses the soft purple petals of the foxglove, and I close my eyes as I lean down to sniff the aroma, one eye cracked to watch him turn back up the path and round the corner behind the bush.

The second he's out of sight, I turn and race off. I turn off the path, between two more bushes, running as fast as I can. There are enough towering plants, trees, topiary, and bushes to help me hide away from their eyes, but one of my shoes falls off, stuck in the mud from the morning showers. My skirt tangles in the brush and snags, but I fight to free it. I have to get out of here.

The phone on my hip, snugly pressed to my skin by my waistband, begins to vibrate, and I know I'm going to run out of time. The edge of the property is just within reach, and I squeeze myself between the pines only to find a towering fence. Impenetrable, not scalable. The black iron bars run parallel, rising up at least four meters, well out of reach. I slide my ankle through and my knee fits, but the bars are narrow, too close to fit my thigh through, let alone my hips.

"Mother of God!" I say, swearing quietly as I peek back into the garden. There are more guards now, searching for me. They have their guns out and raised. I tuck back into the trees and catch my breath. I have to think quickly. Surely, there has to be some way out of this property without climbing this fence. If not, I'm fucked.

The phone on my hip continues to vibrate as I push through the sap-covered fronds dangling from the pine tree. They claw at my face, cling to my hair, and I wince every few seconds as I make my way between the fence and the trees. I reach a corner, where the fence turns to the left, and look before I round it. More guards stand only a few meters away, talking. I hear their hushed voices. They're hunting me.

"Feck's sake," I hiss, and I drop to one knee and pull the phone out of my waistband. If I don't turn it off, they'll hear the vibration. My fingers work to press the power button, but I almost lose my grip and drop it.

My knee grows cold and damp from the moisture in the ground, and I rise slowly and peek out again, not seeing the guards there anymore. I don't know how long I've been out here running around this damn garden evading them, but eventually, they're going to find me. I have to make a run for it, and at the far end of this fence line, I see an opening, a gate, not even shut. I train my eyes on it and press the palm of my hand to my chest, hoping to make my heart stop beating so loudly.

"I am really angry with you, Da," I whisper, then I suck in a breath and dart forward. One foot sinks into the mud, one shoe slapping on the soggy topsoil, but I run. The trees reach out like wardens, attempting to hold me back, and I yelp when I step on a twig with a sharp edge. But the goal is in sight.

My arms pump, my lungs scream for air, and I break out of the tree line into the sunlight to shouts behind me. I'm free. My feet slap the pavement now on the driveway, both shoes now lost to the mud, and all I can think about is finding a safe place away from this house to hide and call my father. Tears burn at my eyes, but I blink them back, and just as I near the end of the driveway, a car screeches up and Declan jumps out.

There's no time to think, no time to evade him. He is right in front of me, and the momentum of my flight can't be stopped. I barrel past him as his arm reaches out, catching me, pulling me back against his chest in a move so jarring it nearly gives me whiplash.

"Where the hell do you think you're going?" Declan's grip is powerful, his arm locked around my waist. I'm heaving for breath, my lungs still burning for air, and he tightens his grip. "What the feckin' hell happened!" His boom of a shout scares me. I jump, but I can't escape him.

"Let me go!" My screech is met with a smack across the face, but it isn't Declan. It's the older man with grey sideburns and tattoos.

"Jaysus, Rian, did you have to?" Declan spins me around, anchored to his hip, then barks, "Get the car parked. You eejits deserve a smack." Then he starts toward the house. I'm his helpless victim again, though this time, he's not as rough as he drags me from the driveway into the house.

Inside, he sets me down and gives me a push. I feel the muzzle of his gun in my back as he grumbles, "Move," and I obey him.

"You can't keep me here. I'm a free woman. I need to get home." I feel the weight of the phone still tucked into my skirt and pray he doesn't know I have it. That he doesn't search me.

"Your Da says otherwise," he snips and gives me another push with the tip of his gun.

At the room, I stomp in, still feeling the squishy mud between my toes. I reel around on him ready to scream, and he's so close to me, I barely have time to think. My hand shoots out and smacks him across the face. I'm angry and scared. I'm supposed to be on a train to nowhere right now, free from this life, this marriage, him. And I'm stuck.

Declan catches my wrist and backs me across the room until my back is pressed into the hard wood of the mantel. I grit my teeth and look him in the eye, unable to turn away. There is more than just anger in his gaze. There's concern there too, as if he might be scared that I could've escaped. Would he be punished? Is that why he's intimidated by that idea? Or is there something more?

"I am trying to keep you safe, Isla."

"Then let me go to my father and leave. I have a plan, Declan." My tone sounds a little too much like pleading, whimpering foolishness. I want to be strong, but the idea of being a prisoner is gutting.

"I am the only one who can protect you now." I'm not sure what his words mean, and I don't want to hear them. I bring my other hand up, away from the phone dangerously tucked away in my skirt, and attempt to slap him again, but he blocks me with the side of his gun as he leans forward, pinning me harder against the mantel.

"The only one," he repeats before his lips cover mine.

The kiss is deep and hungry, the way I imagine we'd have kissed the other day when he walked in on my gown fitting. He's hard against me, chest hammering, breathing ragged as he devours my lips. I'm desperate for breath, but the way his mouth moves against mine is hypnotizing me. He's good at this—really good. He doesn't need to pin my wrists. The way his kiss makes my body feel, I'm glued.

"Christ," I breathe out, and suddenly, I don't want to run from him. Suddenly, I want to go back to that moment when I saw him draped over the back of that chair getting his back stitched up when he was undressing me with his eyes and let him do it for real.

"You're mine," he whispers and then claims my lips again, and I almost believe him.

Almost...

9

DECLAN

Isla doesn't even resist me. She's so pliable in my hands, I set my gun on the mantel and loose her wrists so I can pull her against my body.

When I saw her running, the fright in her eyes, and my arm caught her to my side, my heart nearly exploded. For a split second, I thought I'd lost her, that she'd be off in the streets where the O'Reillys could hunt and kill her. That my chance at redemption was gone, or almost gone, but more than that… that Isla would be gone.

Arranged to marry her, I'd already grown attached to the idea of taking those vows, putting babies in her belly, learning to love her and teaching her to love me. In that moment, everything flashed in front of me and I felt like I lost control, but not now. Not while my lips are on hers, caressing the moans out of her mouth. My hands tug her against my body which is solid and throbbing for her.

The slap didn't even hurt. I see in her eyes the same longing for something more that I've felt not once, but twice in my life. I nearly stole it for myself when I was young, but my cousin offered me a way out, a path to freedom, and I almost took it. I've since had a change of heart, but the longing for more still hovers just below the surface. And Isla's desperation tugs at my heart. I want to show her the things she's missing, the things I missed.

"You're mine, do you hear me? You can't leave this place." I kiss her harder, swallowing the whimper of rebuttal, the way she resists me with her words. But her hands frame in my face and she pulls me closer to herself. She's desperate for me too, her chest heaving.

"Mother of God," she moans as my lips glide across her jawline down to her neck and collarbone. I slide my hands around her back to the zip of her skirt and undo it. It slides to the floor and puddles at her feet, leaving her hips and thighs bare.

"This is mine too," I tell her, rubbing my thumb over the moisture gathering under her silky panties.

"I don't belong to you," she heaves, but she whines when I pinch her clit through the fabric, then she shudders.

"Tell me you don't want me, Isla. Tell me right now that you don't feel this." I push her against the wall, my eyes meeting hers. "Tell me you don't want me as much as I want you." My urge to protect her is overpowered by my need to have her wrapped around my dick, to feel her and experience her warmth as mine and no one else's.

"I... I..." she stutters, her eyes wide with desire and disbelief. "I... I don't... don't want this." Her mouth says she doesn't want me, but the moisture under my touch betrays her.

"If you mean that, I'll turn you out—let Sebastian have his way with you. Is that what you want?" I stroke her through the soggy fabric, and she whimpers. She can't respond because it isn't what she wants.

"I..." She moans again, her eyes squeezing shut. Does she really want to deny us both this? My cock aches for her, as it has done since the night I first laid eyes on her.

"Say it, Isla. Tell me you don't want me and I'll let you go. But if you don't... I'll take what's mine." I lean in closer, my lips brushing hers, inhaling the sweet scent of her arousal.

Isla takes a shaky breath and her gaze meets mine. "I... I don't..." Her voice trails off and she bites her lower lip. It's all the invitation I need.

I crush my lips against hers, punishing her for trying to run. My tongue plunges into her mouth, tasting the sweetness of her tastebuds, the way I've fantasized about a million times. My other hand slips into her panties, two fingers sliding deep inside her wet folds. She's so hot, so wet for me. She moans into my mouth, her hips bucking against my hand.

"That's my girl," I growl, thrusting my fingers in and out. She's so tight, so slick. "I know you want it as much as I do."

"Please..." She whimpers as I pinch her clit. Her knees buckle, but I catch her before she falls to the floor, lifting her up instead. Her leg wraps around my hips as I continue to finger her, loosening her up for what's to come.

"I'm going to fuck you, Isla," I growl against her ear. "And then tomorrow, and the day after that, and every day after that."

Isla whimpers when I pull my fingers out of her and lift her up. Her legs lock around my hips and I carry her to the bed. The door is ajar, but I ignore it, dropping her to the bed and tearing my shirt off. She lies panting, shuddering, until I slip my fingers into the crotch of her panties and pull them down. Then she inches backward over the bed as if evading me.

My belt clinks as I unfasten it, then shove my pants down. I kick off my shoes, step out of the pants, and crawl across the bed where she cowers.

"I said I don't want this," she says plainly, but her eyes lock on my hard dick.

"Your eyes say you do. And your pussy drips with liquid gold for me, Princess." My fingers inch up under her blouse and find her bra a barrier to what I crave. I nestle between her spread legs, and she sucks in a breath as my cock dips into her juices. "Tell me to stop and I will..." Our eyes meet, and she bites her lip. I grab her tit through the lace of her bra, and she gasps, but she doesn't say a word.

I slide into her moisture slowly, stretching her. Isla arches her back up, whimpering, then clenches around me tightly.

"Holy mother," she mumbles, and I take it that she likes what she's feeling.

"You're mine, Isla," I say, my voice deep and guttural. "Don't ever forget it." Then I plunge into her heated depths, claiming her.

She moans, but not in protest. No, she moans because she likes it. "You feel so fucking good, Isla."

Her nails dig into my back as I thrust in and out, her legs locked around my hips like we were made for each other. My name falls from her lips in a litany of moans, whimpers, and pleas for more.

It annoys me that I can't feel her flesh, so I tear her shirt down the front. The fabric frays and splits open, and she gasps and clings to it, but I shove it away. "God, I need to feel you against my body," I tell her in a low growl. I pry her hands back and pin them over her head with one hand, then unhook the clasp for her front-hook bra and bare her chest.

Her eyes track to mine again as I drink her in and squeeze her fleshy globes one at a time. "Fuck, you're so sexy."

"And you're a monster," she hisses, but her hips arch upward, begging for more.

"I am," I admit, thrusting hard. "And now you're my pet."

She moans again, and I know she yields to me. "Say it," I growl as I reach for the belt on the bedpost. "Say you're mine."

"I'm yours..." She pants, then moans again.

"Who are you?" I ask, lifting her hips higher then, slamming into her again.

"Yours," she whimpers, her legs shaking.

"Tell me you're mine."

I slap her ass, and she yelps.

"I'm yours," she gasps, her eyes dazed. "I'm yours."

"And?" I ask, pumping into her harder.

"I... I... belong to you." She's so close, her orgasm just a few thrusts away.

"Good girl," I praise her, then drive deep inside her again.

"Oh, God," she screams as her orgasm tears through her. Her legs wrap around me with an unyielding strength, and her inner muscles clench with a fervent intensity, holding me tightly in a hot vise.

"That's my girl," I praise her as my own release builds. "You belong to me." I smack her ass again, and she screams louder.

"Say it again," I demand, then slap her other cheek.

"I... I..." She pants, then moans as I spank her again. "I belong to you."

"That's my good girl." I praise her, then slam inside her one last time. "I..." I groan, then my seed spurts into her. With long, slow thrusts, I continue pumping into her, gripping her hip and claiming her lips in a heated kiss again. She's yielded now, allowing me to move with fluidity and freedom. Her body grows limp under me.

We both pant and catch our breaths as my cock softens inside her. Isla's eyes meet mine, and for the first time, I don't see hatred in them. I see acceptance. I hover over her, wishing I could take the weight of this situation off both of our shoulders so we could have a chance to learn what it means to fall in love instead of being shoved together like two jigsaw puzzle pieces that don't fit.

"I wish you wouldn't fight me. There are forces at play that you know nothing about, things no one has told you. I need to protect you, Aisling." I rub the tip of my nose across hers, and she blinks slowly then turns her head away from me. "I don't like this any more than you do, but you know you're mine now."

"For now," she says calmly, and I don't know what she means by it, but she's wrong. This isn't a temporary thing. Isla O'Connor is permanently my property now, and there is nothing she or anyone else except her father can do about it.

I pull out, backing away. The interchange between us is cold now, the heat of our passion dying down. She rolls to her side and stares at the pile of her clothing on the floor. I'd get it for her, but I like her there naked on the bed. I dress slowly and watch her as she blinks lazily, seems groggy.

We're not that different. Her heart to run, my thirst for freedom. It's a kindred spirit thing we share, something no one told us we had to share or forced upon either of us. And while I may be getting the better end of the deal here, there is still a lot for her to embrace and enjoy.

"I'll send dinner..." I tell her as I button the last few buttons on my shirt.

"Not hungry," comes her reply, but I know she'll eat. She always does.

"I'll come back later." When I step into the hallway, Rian is there waiting. I give him orders not to let her outside again, then scold him for turning his back on her for a single second. We lock her in and he follows me downstairs.

Isla won't be trying to run again because she's under lock and key now. I just wish there were a way I could convince her the locks are there for her protection and not to imprison her, so I could let her be free too. One day, I will. For now, I have to do what I have to do.

10

ISLA

I'm cold, but lying here shivering in the air conditioning after being covered in sweat from the run and that romp feels good. It feels better than the numb ache hollowing me out inside. I lie perfectly still, afraid to break the trance I'm under. Relaxation has gripped my body, moves through every cell, snaking its way through my core and up to my chest and back again.

Declan is a master at owning me. I have to admit I loved what he did, how he dominated me, forced the truth of my desire for him to come out. I want him. I can't keep it a secret. Maybe I should never have tried to. Part of me loves how he possesses me body, soul, and spirit, but part of me hates myself.

The girlish crush I have on him is disgusting. Men like him are animals, taking what they want and getting away with it. I should hate him, be repulsed by the way he thinks he can walk right in here and bed me without consent. But I can't. I've had eyes for him for years, and I never told a single soul except Rebecca.

I roll to my stomach and turn my head so my eyes remain fixed on my clothing across the room. I feel his sex drain from my body and think how differently things could have gone. Perhaps I'd still dislike him or resist the marriage that's supposed to happen between us, but had he asked me to dinner, at least tried to woo me in a natural way, maybe this would feel different. Maybe I wouldn't feel like I was losing myself to something I'd never come back from.

I push myself up from the mattress and stare at my feet. The moisture between my thighs disgusts me but reminds me of how giddy his body made me feel. I want to wash him off me, but I want to pull him back in, feel his strength, revel in the pillar of safety I felt the moment he told me I belong to him now. Why did it do that to me? Why am I so weak?

Forcing myself to my feet, I feel weak in the knees. I stand for a moment before walking, moving toward the clothing on the floor. The phone is there, hidden in the pile of cloth that is now soiled with mud and sweat. I'm sure they're still looking for it, and I may only have a few minutes longer with it. I can't waste the precious time lying around sulking about the best sex of my life.

I rifle through the skirt and find the phone tangled in the dirty material, then I walk to the dresser and pull out fresh underwear, a camisole, and some shorts. With a glance toward the door, I slip into the bathroom and shut it. There's no lock, but I can run the hot water as a cover for the noise.

I quickly wash myself in a whore's bath, then dress and turn on the shower water before I sit on the closed toilet and dial my father's number. He picks up on the third ring.

"Mick here, what can I do for you?"

"Da," I whimper, and it's the first hint of weakness I've allowed myself to truly display. "It's Isla."

"Aisling, God's graces, how are you?" he asks. He sounds frantic as I hear a muffled, "Brennan, it's her."

"I'm okay, Da. How is Mum?" My hand trembles. I'm shaking like a leaf in a hurricane waiting for them to burst in and take the phone from me. I know they'll be furious, but it's not like I'm arranging a coup. I'm calling my family to let them know I'm okay.

"Mum is worried, Rebecca too. We're fine, Aisling. Are you okay? How is he treating you?" Da sounds worried, but not overly so. I know he's had a longstanding relationship with the O'Rourke family, though I'm not sure to what extent he's involved. Da is a good man, not a criminal like these men who hold me hostage. I'm sure his debts weren't even his fault, a bad loan or a mistake of some kind.

"He's a kind man, Da," I tell him, and while Declan hasn't laid a hand on me, I'm not sure I believe myself. The way he pinned me to that mattress showed me the beast inside him, though I can't deny how much I enjoyed it.

"Good, good, Isla," he says, switching to my more intimate name, the one I prefer. "This isn't the way I wanted this. You know that, right?"

"I know, Da." My sense of duty to my family is strong. It always has been. That's why I stole, to make sure my family could be protected and provided for. I can still follow my plan. I can still make us disappear if my father goes along with it. "Da?"

"Yes, Princess?"

"Da, I want you and Mum to pack a bag. Rebecca too. I want you to be ready. When I come to you, we'll run, okay? We can get away from these men and their wars and—"

The door bursts open, startling me, and the hairy, tattooed man stands over me with a glare. "Give me my phone, ya bleedin' banshee." He reaches out and grabs for it before I can even finish my sentence. I don't know what he heard, but I don't want to give it up. I hold onto it tightly and pull back.

"No, I need to speak to my father." My hand wrestles against his until I'm standing, fighting him off, and he smacks me hard. It stuns me, causing me to stumble backward and bump into the wall. It also makes me relinquish my grip on the phone as I reach to cover my stinging cheek.

I can't believe he just did that. My mind is reeling even as Declan barges in and shoves the man out of the bathroom with a shout.

He turns to me and cups my cheek, the pad of his thumb brushing over my lip which stings now. I taste the faint hint of copper on my tongue and know the man busted my lip.

"Are you okay?" he asks, stormy green seas raging as he peers into my eyes. I nod and lick the blood from my lip. "Isla, you shouldn't have done that."

I nod again, not even knowing the right response. I feel like I'm on a yo-yo, in his arms begging for him to pleasure me one minute, terrified and being struck the next, then back in his arms wondering why my world is spinning out of control the next. He's here. I feel safe, but I feel trapped. But I want him here, and still I want to push him away.

Declan presses a soft kiss to my lips and as he backs away, I see a spot of blood on his lip before he licks it away. "I'll deal with him. You just get ready for dinner." He touches my lip again with his thumb, and for some stupid reason, I ache inside when he walks away.

I hear the shouting and angry voices in the hallway as I sink down the wall onto the bathroom floor and hug my knees to my chest. If I were the sort of woman who cried and wailed like a banshee, now would be the time that I'd do it. But I'm not.

I'm the sort of woman who thinks carefully, plans wisely, and moves with purpose.

I just don't know what way to move now.

11

DECLAN

Ronan's eyes are dark and angry, almost black, clouded with hesitation as he looks at me. With doubt. Rage surges through my body over the position I'm still in with him. It's true what they say. You can do a million correct things and no one notices, but you fuck a goat once and they'll call you "One Goat" the rest of your life. My mistake of listening to Eamon, being lured away even in my thoughts for just a split second of my life, will haunt me forever.

"It's got to be dealt with, Declan." Ro's voice is as thunderous as his gaze. Brynn had absolutely no reason to march into my brother's office and try to smear my name. The way I handled Mick was on par with every other instance of interaction. My younger counterpart is a fool, and I know my own brother can see it, but the rest of the family won't always side with Ronan and his mercy.

Yes, I fucked up by allowing myself to believe our cousin's lies, but I didn't act up on those deceptive thoughts. Still, the one time I met with him in secret, where I didn't slit his throat the way I should have, and it hangs over me like an omen, a predictor of my potential future behavior. Behavior Brynn thinks he will prevent if Ronan cuts me out of the family now. Brynn is about to learn a lesson in loyalty.

"I'll deal with it," I grumble, wise enough to know if I attempt to unleash any of my anger right now, it will make me appear out of control, and that's the last thing I need. Ronan has me walking a tightrope here. Isla O'Connor and the alliance formed by our wedding is my future. Marrying her family to ours will establish the O'Rourkes in new territories and quash disputes that have been simmering below the surface for decades. Everything is in place to make that happen, and when it does, Ronan will see that I'm in this for the long haul.

I turn to head to the door and Ronan calls after me, "Today, Declan."

My shoulders tighten at the order. I know the weasel is here in this house, probably just down the hallway. I'll pass him on my way to Ronan's living room where my younger brother Connor watches over Isla, who I brought with me to avoid another incident like the one a few weeks ago when she ran.

I'm grateful for Ronan's belief in me despite my failure, but I know the rest of the family won't see it that way. Brynn is a rat and a nark, going behind my back to accuse me of slacking off, of turning my back on my duty as an enforcer. Ronan doesn't take things like this lightly, and I'm surprised he is allowing me to handle it instead of taking matters into his own hands. It makes me think there may still be more doubt in his mind about my fealty than I thought.

The hall is dark, doors to each room on either side of the hall closed. The house is cool too, giving off a foreboding sense. I see the light streaming from the room at the far end of the hall on the lefthand side, where Isla and my brother sit waiting, and I see a form moving in the dark in my direction. The silhouette isn't hard to distinguish. It's Brynn.

"What the actual fuck do you think you're doing going to Ronan like that?" My growl comes rumbling up my chest and out my mouth at the same time my arm draws back and I make a fist. A hard right hook into Brynn's gut forces air out of his lungs and doubles him over. He grips his stomach and coughs, gasping for breath as I bring my elbow down hard on the back of his head.

"You're lucky he didn't cut your tongue out for narking." He wants an enforcer? Well, I'll be an enforcer of our family's true laws and morals. We stick together and believe in one another. That's a fact that has never changed.

Brynn drops to his knees still coughing and sucking in air like he's a drowning man just revived. I stand over him, wishing I could kick him in the gut, but I know when to draw the line. This is nothing more than a chastisement. I won't cross that line and be called a traitor for attacking one of our own, not after my almost-mistake. I know how to teach a man a lesson, and that is what Brynn needs—to learn a lesson.

"Fecking hell," he gasps, and I knee him in the face, making him fall backward against the wall where he plops down and shakes his head.

"Do it again and I'll slit your throat myself, but not before cutting your snake's tongue out of your mouth. In this family we remain loyal, and your little visit puts a target on your back." I'm glaring at him, but in the darkness, I can't even make out his expression. There's no way he can even see my features, but I know he felt those blows, and I hope to God that he gets the point.

I leave him sitting there heaving and prowl the rest of the way down the hallway to see Connor approaching the door. He looks alarmed, likely having heard the way I struck Brynn. I hold up a hand to him and nod. "It's fine... Just a little discipline session." My eyes flick to Isla who has her arms crossed over her chest, staring out the window. She looks annoyed and bored, but she's still beautiful. "How was she?"

"Well, Princess Whinge-Bag is as feisty as ever." Connor chuckles as he turns to glance at her and then back to me. "But she wasn't a problem. Good luck taming that shrew, eejit." He shakes his head and slaps my shoulder as he walks past me. "I'm right glad you're on the chopping block and not me."

Connor's passing comment irritates me, but I'm glad too. He has no clue what he's missing by not seeing Isla for everything she is. He sees only her complaining and anger, and he doesn't understand it because he's never had a disloyal thought in his life. Unlike me and Isla, Connor has always wanted to live this life. He loved it the moment our father started grooming him to become our logistics officer. He can't understand what it feels like to be forced to stay when your heart screams for freedom.

"Did he treat you well?" I ask her softly, and the flash of anger in her eyes as she looks up at me tells me what I need to know. She probably spent this entire time while I was meeting with Ronan complaining and bitching, and Connor probably put her in her place a few times.

"Can we leave now? And can I call my father, please? I want to hear how my family is doing." Isla rises and smooths the cream-colored fabric of her skirt down her legs. I let my eyes wander across her curves to her feet and then back up to her face. The way her light blue blouse hugs her tits is attractive.

"Come," I tell her, and I jerk my head toward the door. When we walk back through the hallway and out the front door, I notice Brynn peeling himself off the floor with Connor's help. No doubt, he'll go squealing like a sow to the first fifty people he sees, and he'll be doing me a favor, reinforcing that I'm the one who lays down the law in this family, and they'll all start to get the picture that I'm not to be fucked with.

"Your phone?" Isla asks, trailing behind me as we descend the steps toward my car. Nicholas has the engine running, waiting for us to climb in, but he knows better than to get out and open the door when I've had a meeting with my older brother. I'm never in a good mood.

"Later," I grumble again, and I open the door for her to climb in. She stands obstinately and stomps her foot.

"Now. It's been weeks since I've spoken with them and I'd like to know how they're doing." Her severe expression doesn't move me, though her stubbornness does annoy me some.

"Someone burned one of their outbuildings down and they lost a few sheep. They're fine. I have my men there. Now, get in the car."

I leave no room in my order for her to resist me, so she climbs in but not before glaring at me coldly. I roll my neck around and stretch my shoulders before climbing into the car and tapping on the dividing wall. Nicholas takes the hint and pulls the car forward as I shut the door.

"Is this how you'll treat me once we're married? Like a prisoner?" Isla really is feisty today. I like her spunk. I just don't like how she's taking her anger out on me as if I have any choice in this situation either.

"If you were my wife, you'd be on your knees with my cock down your throat right now," I tell her as I loosen my tie. She scoffs as I stare out the window. This attitude and snark isn't exactly the sort of personality I thought I'd be marrying myself to, either. She could go a long way toward being more attractive as a mate if she were a little less bitchy.

"You're lucky I don't seduce you just to put that slug in my mouth and bite it off."

Her biting comment opens the dam I've had holding back the worst of my anger over Brynn's narking, and my hand shoots out, grabbing her by the back of her neck with a hefty grip on her tangled waves. She gasps as I pull her toward me with so much force her body lurches off the seat and her knees land on the floor at my feet.

"Say it again," I threaten, and her eyes go wide with fright. "Go ahead and tell me who you really are, Isla, because I want to know who I'm marrying. You think I like this?"

I expect her to cower, to cry, to whimper and plead for me to let her go, but this shrew isn't broken easily. She tries to shake her head, and her scowl only deepens as she chokes out, "You like fucking me..."

Her comment takes me by surprise because she's right. I do like fucking her. I like it enough that I'm going soft, allowing myself to see her as a lady and not as a job, which is what this is supposed to be. But I'm not a monster, not the sort of man who just uses a woman as a means to an end and then tosses her aside, and Isla isn't a tool or a bargaining chip.

The uncertainty in her eyes, I've seen it before when I looked in the mirror. I've felt it. As rebellious as she is, as insistent that we are forcing her against her will, as much as she wants to run away and not fulfill her duty in this arrangement, I find myself drawn to her. I should abhor her disloyalty, but I find a common thread running through my own heart and I can't deny it.

My lips close over hers as she gasps and pushes my chest away. I kiss her hard, claiming that intimacy for us, desperate to prove to her that we are the same, that in our hearts, we are one and we haven't even spoken the vows thrust on us. Isla's hands beat at my chest for a moment, her struggling, muffled, vocalized rejection swallowed by my kisses until she softens and rests her hands on my biceps.

Then she kisses me back, no longer pushing me away but now pulling my lapels toward her. Her kiss grows hungrier, devouring my attention. Her hands move to my thighs, and I tighten my grip on her hair as she rises and straddles me. I pull her mouth hard against mine and don't give her a second of reprieve to breathe. My dick is swelling, demanding to be in her and show her how alike we really are.

"Mother of God," she breathes when I let my lips trail down her throat to the hollow near her collarbone. I suck it and bite the soft flesh as she reaches for my belt buckle and begins to undo my pants. I feel her pulse beneath my lips and relish it as she works the zip of my pants.

I want to tell her all the ways I can make her life everything she hopes it will be, but unless she sees it with her own eyes—that she'll be happier and safer here in this family than anywhere else—she'll never believe me. I have to show her, and I'm starting right now.

"You're a damn right wagon," I growl then bite her collar bone, not hard enough to draw blood, but enough that she hisses.

"Feckin' cunt, just own me already." Her neediness comes across in panting breaths, groping hands, writhing hips as she frees my hard dick and strokes it. She palms my balls in one hand as she strokes me. The sensations are incredible.

My hand reaches beneath her skirt, and I feel the moisture there, rubbing it with the back of my pointer finger as my other hand still mercilessly clutches her hair. I hook a finger through the crotch of her panties, and with one hard pull, I split them so the fabric parts and her core is exposed to me. Then I thrust my finger in and she hisses, turning her mouth back down to steal another kiss.

Her pussy is hot and wet, clenching around my finger as she strokes my cock. I add another while her tongue dances with mine, her hands fisting my shirt, digging into my chest. "God, I'm gonna fuckin' wreck you," I growl, knowing full well that she'll only ever be mine now.

"I know," she whines as she grinds against my hand. Her pussy rubs against my palm as my fingers sink into her. Her eagerness urges me onward.

She's so damn responsive, so ready for me. I pull my fingers out of her and line up my shaft, pressing the head against her entrance. She moans into my mouth as I begin to push in. Slowly, agonizingly slowly, I breach her. Her walls clench around me, the tightness almost too much.

"Jaysus, you're so feckin' tight," I groan. I pull back slightly and plunge back in again, this time burying myself a little deeper. As I do, the car rocks over a pothole and my cock slams into her back wall, making her hiss. Her nails dig into my skin as she arches her back, taking more of me inside her. "That's it, love," I coax her. "Take every inch of me."

Isla is a blubbering mess, shuddering and riding me, rising and falling as I thrust into her. My thumb finds her clit, and I rub it in circles as my other hand fists her hair, guiding her mouth back to mine. Her moans vibrate in my mouth, her pussy squeezing me tighter with every stroke.

"That's right, moan for me," I tell her between kisses. "Show me how much you want this." I give her every inch of my length now, thrusting hard and making sure she feels it.

"I... I... Holy mother, I want you." Her words are punctuated by the hard collision of our bodies connecting as we fuck each other senseless. My hand is crushed between us, but I don't relent.

"Say it again," I growl, pressing my thumb harder against her clit. She's twitching, jolting, soaking wet for more.

"I want you," she whimpers, and her hot walls contract around me, so tightly I know she's breaking loose.

"Say it again, Isla. Say you're mine," I demand, my thrusts becoming more urgent as I feel my own orgasm crashing down on me. My balls draw up and the pressure builds. Her mere words will send me toppling over the edge into the abyss of ecstasy, and I'm only waiting to hear her utter the syllables I need to hear.

"I'm yours, Declan," she cries out as her body shatters around me, milking my cock with her tight pussy.

With a low growl of pleasure and possession, I fill her with my seed, marking her as mine. She continues to rise and fall, slicking my length with more silky moisture. I grab her ass now, pulling her down harder on me so I can feel her warmth on every inch of my shaft. She shudders and continues to twitch as her lips return to mine. I kiss her hard and bite her lip. Fucking her into silence wasn't my plan, but it worked.

When her body tenses and she pushes against my shoulders, straightening, I suck in a breath and rest my head backward on the seat. Her pupils are dilated, lips kiss-swollen and red. Her hair is mussed, her chest heaving for air, and my cock is still deliciously buried inside her, feeling her rapid pulse throb against my tender shaft.

"Just because I like fucking you doesn't mean I want to marry you," she says plainly, and I take her point. I really like fucking her, and she'll spread those legs for me any time I ask. It's unspoken, but I see it in her eyes.

"But that pussy of yours..." I lick my lips and smirk at her, and I watch her fight a smirk. Her walls tighten on me briefly, and she looks away as she slides off my lap, leaving a puddle of sex on my pelvis.

"It's mine... and I still want to call my father—" she says, but her words are cut off by the sound of tires squealing and then a rapid *pop-pop-pop* of gunfire. The car lurches, shocking us.

"Christ," she gasps, ducking down. I'm instantly on alert, and the divider between driver and passenger cabins in the limo goes down.

"We have company..." Nicholas sounds stressed. His eyes show alarm in the reflection in the mirror.

I reach into my holster, pinned under my coat on my chest, and pull out my weapon. Goosebumps rise on my arms. "Who is it? How many cars?"

It has to be Sebastian. There is no one else who would come after me so brazenly. The winding road between my home and Ronan's is safe. It always has been. It means they've laid a trap. They've been waiting.

"Two cars, sir..." The car lurches again from side to side as Nicholas tries to keep the pursuers from coming alongside us. "I can't outrun them," he shouts, and I hear the growing panic in his tone. This is the worst thing that could've happened.

"Fecking hell," I growl. This isn't good. Isla is exposed out here on the road, and if she hadn't been so stupid as to try to escape last time, I'd have left her at home where she was safer. Behind reinforced walls and iron gates.

"What's happening?" she asks, but I don't get the chance to answer. Another volley of rounds strikes the car and we are suddenly spinning, toppling around and around. I shouldn't have brought her out.

Now I'm going to lose her...

12

ISLA

The look of alarm on Declan's face is frightening. The car is stopped, lying on its top. I'm pinned against the shattered window as I hear his driver calling for help on a radio. Declan struggles to fasten his pants. His weapon lies on the roof next to him in a puddle of glass shards.

"What happened?" I ask in a daze, my head throbbing. I touch my forehead lightly and feel dampness. When I pull my fingers away, I see crimson. I'm hurt.

"Stay here," Declan barks. "And whatever you do, don't scream. They probably don't know you're in here." He scoots closer to the window next to me that's busted out. There are a few windows still intact, and by the grace of God, they're tinted. Maybe no one will see me.

Dread floods every cell in my being as I reach for him. "Don't leave me," I whimper, feeling genuinely terrified. Whoever is out there shot up the car, caused us to flip. I heard there are two cars too, and with just Declan and his driver, we're outnumbered. "Please," I plead. I'm shaking, scared to death. I may piss myself in fear.

"Isla, please." Declan reaches into his boot and pulls out a tiny revolver. His eyes are intense as he grips my chin and locks gazes with me. "Do you know how to shoot?"

My eyes bounce back and forth between his and I nod. "Yes, why? I don't want to shoot. You said you'd protect me." I'm confused, overwhelmed. My mind is racing. I'm not a killer. I'm just an accountant.

"Take this," he says, thrusting it into my hand. He releases his grip on my face and tells me, "Don't let them take you. Do you understand me? You use this. You shoot and shoot and if you run out of ammunition, you run. Do you hear me?"

I'm numb. His words aren't making sense. I was just fucked senseless, then endured a car accident. I'm lightheaded, bleeding, gasping for breath. My body hasn't even registered the pain, but I know I'm injured.

"Isla!" he shouts, and I blink a few times. "Do you understand me?"

I nod once, and he kisses me hard before hastily pulling away and crawling out the window. It's only a matter of seconds before I hear gunfire. I'm wincing, trembling and cowering in this overturned limo, scared for my life. I can't just sit here and wait. I'm a sitting duck. He said to stay inside but if they reach into this limo with their weapons, I'm dead.

So I push myself up on my hands and knees and crawl to the window. Glass presses into my palm on one hand, my knuckles on the hand holding the gun. I peek out the broken glass and see nothing, but the report of gunfire is loud, deafening. The gun is loaded, six rounds in the revolver with the safety set to off. I stick my head out the window and breathe in the scent of gasoline. I can't stay here risking an explosion, either.

"Help," I whimper under my breath, but there is no help. No one is coming. I'm alone out here with men who are hunting me. I know they came for me, not him. I know this is the O'Reilly crew here to clean up the mess I made. Declan says they want me dead. They'll never take me alive, and I have to fight for my life—for my father's life.

I hear shouting too, Declan and his driver, male voices I don't know. They're speaking in Gaeilge, which I barely know. But I pick up certain words like "slaughter" and "debt". It only confirms they're here for me as I wriggle out of the mangled wreckage and scramble to the side of the car. The sounds are louder out here, more terrifying.

My body trembles as I grip the weapon, now better able to hear and see what's going on. From my vantage point, I see two SUVs with all four doors open. Eight men at least, maybe ten or more. But I see a few bodies on the ground, men bleeding and writhing, a few as still as death. Declan really is fighting for me, and for himself too. I brought this on him, and now guilt consumes me for what I've done. I don't want him to die.

"Hand her over, O'Rourke, and we won't kill you." The angry voice is barely distinguishable as he switches from Gaeilge to English and back, slurring insults.

"Feck off to hell," Declan screams, and more gunfire erupts. When it silences, I hear the sound of men grunting and tussling.

In the distance, the tree line, I see a path into the woods. It looks like salvation, but it's at least a hundred meters there. I'd be completely exposed, and I don't know what's on the other side, how far the woods go. My feet seem untrustworthy right at this moment. I'm not sure I can even walk, let alone run, not when men are shooting at me.

My hands continue to shake as I slowly rise up and peer over the belly of the car. Declan is locked in a fistfight with someone, a man with an angry tattoo on the left side of his face, and his driver is prone on the ground. Two men, glowering with jade-colored eyes, stalk toward me.

"Don't let them take you," Declan told me. *"Just shoot and shoot and shoot."*

A tiny whimper rises to the surface, but I fight it back. I won't let them take me. I can't. They'll kill me. They've seen that I'm here and they are coming, and I know what it means.

Shooting to my feet, I aim the gun at one of the men and start shooting. The gun bounces in my grip, missing him with the first shot, but I fire again and again. The bullets tear through his chest, hitting center mass, and my shaking arms only barely hold the gun steady. I turn to the second man, who is now in a dead sprint, only a few strides toward me, and I shoot him once, but it only grazes his side. The impending doom I feel as the gun clicks but no more rounds discharge almost cripples me. I turn to run.

Two strides...

Three...

And he's on me, tackling me to the ground with such force it knocks the air from my lungs. I screech and roll, attempting to fight him off, but his hand comes down on my face hard, smacking me.

"Stop it! No! Let me go!" I fight, clawing and swinging my arms, but he's stronger than me, double my size. He smacks me again and then grabs me by the hair and stands up, dragging me along with him.

"Lookie what I found," he announces proudly. My knees scrape the pavement as he moves, and I cling to his leg in an attempt to stop some of the pain. My teeth sink into his pants leg, finding his meaty calf and biting down hard. He yelps and kicks me, sending me flailing and rolling across the pavement until my body slams into something hard. It's Declan, on his knees, a gun to his head.

"Damn cunt," the man curses, and I scramble away from him, clinging to Declan. He's stiff and stoic, rigid. Not moving. His chin is high and his chest heaves.

"I'm sorry," he says softly. The man with the gun to his head nudges him.

"Thought you could keep the princess here safe, did ye?" The man is ugly, beady, inky eyes and a nasty scar in his right eyebrow. I hate him instantly, and it makes me want to plead for Declan's life.

"He did nothing. Please, just take me. I'm what you want." My words come out choked. I'm still dizzy, now almost desperate for the pain to consume me. My vision is dim. I probably took a knock to the head.

"Oh, believe me, we'll take you," one of them says while grabbing his dick through his pants. They both chuckle, and I feel Declan tense further. I'm so in tune with him now, so one with him that all I can sense is how angry he is, how focused he is on protecting me. His hand laces around my wrist and he grips it.

"You want to hurt someone, hurt me. Leave her out of this. She's learned her lesson and she's going straight." The way his body rumbles as he speaks moves me. I wrap my arms around him and shake. On his stomach, I feel moisture, and I look down. A crimson blossom there tells me he's been injured too—the car or a knife, maybe a bullet. It sickens me. I feel nausea making my stomach roil as much as the spinning in my head.

"That's not how this works. Sebastian will love to see both of your heads on a platter. You should've known better than to protect her, Declan." The man with the gun nudges his head again, and I wince.

"Stop it! Leave him alone," I plead. Angry, hot tears threaten me, but I force them back. I'm not a baby. I'm not a weak, defenseless woman. "Just take me," I tell them, standing up, but Declan grips my wrist harder and I wobble.

"A lot of people will pay for your sins, Princess." There it is again, that name he calls me. The one so many people have called me. I hate it. I'm not a fucking pawn in someone's hellish nightmare of a game they're playing.

"Yeah, well I wouldn't piss on you if you were afire," I tell him harshly and wince when he draws his hand back as if to strike me, but the blow never comes. The other man stays his arm. Instead, he reaches again for his groin and this time goes to undo his belt.

"What if we just have our way right here on the street... right in front of your betrothed? You want to insult me again, bitch?" I shudder just thinking of that, of his hands on me the way Declan's hands were just on me. I realize then that I don't want any other man's hands on me ever. Never again. Only Declan's.

"Screw you... Fecking bastards."

He reaches for me again, tearing me away from Declan's grasp. He's defenseless. He can't do anything. With a gun to his head, if he moves, they'll kill him and then me. He has no choice but to wait, and I'm not going to wait around to see what they do. I come out swinging, launching myself into his chest and pounding his sides.

When he shoves me back, I fall to the ground hard, but just in time. A new rain of bullets falls, this time from a few cars approaching on the horizon. I curl into a ball and cover my head, whimpering, until I feel warmth and weight cover me.

"I'm here. Stay down. Stay still... Ronan is here," Declan says, his words soothing me.

"Oh, God," I breathe, feeling relief wash over me but still terrified. I want to fall apart, to cling to him and let myself feel safe, but the sheer terror of what I've just been through numbs me. I lie there listening to more gunfire, what sounds like an explosion as another car crashes, and then calm.

Too calm.

Dead calm.

Declan slides off me, and I feel myself being lifted.

My eyes squeak open. The two men are dead, in puddles of blood on the ground between us and the new car that came to our rescue. I'm in Declan's arms, surrounded by Ronan's men, all armed and angry.

"Cleaners are on the way. Get the package to safety," Ronan barks.

"Aye," Declan grumbles, and I'm confused again. "Package." "Princess." What does it all mean?

Then suddenly, we're in a new car, zooming away from the scene of the accident. I don't know what happened. I don't know why they're so angry with me, after me like this. Why just returning the money wouldn't be enough. But I feel safe. I'm on his lap, in his arms, his lips pressing kisses to my temple.

"You're bleeding," Declan says softly, smoothing a finger over my forehead.

"So are you," I say, remembering the blossom of blood on his stomach.

"Just a cut. I'm okay." His eyes focus earnestly on my face, and he brushes my cheek with his palm, then cups it. "Are you alright?"

His question is ridiculous. Of course I'm not alright. I killed a man. But I nod. My father taught me to hunt and shoot and skin a sheep. The blood doesn't bother me. It's the guilt over what I've done. Over what I'm capable of doing. That I can be like these monsters.

"You... I'm..." I can't form words. The adrenaline is still thrumming through me, my vision still dim. I feel I may pass out any second.

"Shh, I'm here." Declan presses his lips to my forehead, and when he pulls away, there is blood on them. I let my eyes flutter shut and sleep claims me.

When I open them, I feel cold. I'm lying on his bed—not my bed. Not the place he keeps me locked away from the world. His bed, in his room, with his whiskey and gun on the nightstand. His firm, large body is on the mattress beside me. His hand is pressing a damp cloth to my skin in what I can only assume is his attempt to clean me after the ordeal. I look up at him, and he smiles softly.

"There you are." His whisper is soft and gentle, but I know because I've seen what he's capable of. The gentleness inside this man is what pulls me into him like gravity. The harsher reality of his potential is what pushes me away.

"I..." I want to speak, but I still don't trust my voice.

"Just a cut, no big deal. From the glass. Doctor says you're fine. You might have a mild concussion, which would explain why you've been sleeping for eighteen hours." He pressed the cloth to my face again, and I shift, feeling the covers against my bare skin. I'm naked, probably stripped off to make sure there were no more injuries. "And you'll have bruising. We took a hard tumble. But you're alive."

The crash, the gunfight. It's not news to me. I'm not shocked by remembering it because I've done nothing but dream horrible, awful things the entire time I was sleeping.

"You saved me..." I whisper.

"I told you. You need my protection. Now will you let me care for you?" His hand draws my chin up, and I blink slowly as I process it all. I've already given my consent for this wedding, but my plan to run still burns hot in my chest. If those men would come after me like that, how will Declan protect my father? He can't be in two places at once, and it's only a matter of time until Sebastian goes after my family.

"I'll be right back," he says as his phone starts to ring.

I shudder at the lack of warmth as he slides off the bed and brings his phone to his ear. He steps into the hallway, but I can hear him say, "The package is safe... No worries... just a bump. Yes... I gave you my word. The wedding is still on..."

As he walks away, I find myself being drawn into sleep again, wondering what it all means. Why do they call me a package? Or is there something else at play here? I want to think it through but I can't, not when sleep tugs me back to the harrowing depths of terror and darkness.

I have to get out of here…

13

DECLAN

My phone is at two percent, beeping at me as I end the call. I slide it into my pocket and turn back to the room, but from the crack in the doorway I see Isla is sleeping again. Maeve sits in the chair just outside the room where I asked her to. Ronan's partner is a fantastic doctor, but I feel like Isla is going to need more than just bandages this time. The expression in her eyes—the shock and panic—it's still there. This is fucking with her head.

"Thank you, Maeve," I tell her, knowing my older brother is downstairs.

She nods and offers an expression of sympathy. "I'll go in and sit with her, be here if she wakes up." Ronan sent her to my home the instant they heard there was an accident. She was here only moments after we arrived and I laid Isla in bed. Now he waits downstairs for me, and based on that short call with him, I know he's not happy.

"Thank you. I'll send Sera to bring you fresh cloths for that cut. Without stitches, I think it's going to keep bleeding." I'm more concerned for her mental wellbeing than the cut, though she'll probably have a nasty scar.

"Finn will be here with anesthetic and my suture kit, Declan." Maeve stands and rests a hand on my bicep. Her compassionate bedside manner is comforting to me, especially in such a hostile world where men expect one another to buck up under loads like this and never show weakness. Isla shouldn't have to be treated like that. I'm grateful Ronan's wisdom in choosing a surgeon as a mate has helped bring some of those feminine touches to our family, the ones we lost when Mum died.

"Thank you," I tell her, and I nod as I turn toward the stairs. It pains me to leave Isla, but after such a brazen attack like that, we have to do something. Sebastian is bold as hell thinking he can blow my car off the road and get away with it.

Our cleaners will make it look like a two-car accident, and my limo is probably already in the crusher waiting to be melted down. Eight of his men are dead, and Nicholas is off at the hospital for observation. I'm livid and despite my own injuries, I'm not slowing down.

My feet carry me into the living room where Ronan and Connor stand talking. Their eyes perk up as I enter, and Ronan asks, "How is she?"

I have to swallow the knot in my throat and clear it with a cough. "Maeve says she has a concussion and a nasty gash, but she's fucked up, Ro. Women should never see shit like that." I walk straight to my liquor cabinet and pull out three tumblers, filling each of them with Writer's Tears, then nodding at them with my back to my brothers. They join me, and each of them picks up a glass. We drink in silence.

To think how close I came to destroying everything all because I have this incessant need to prove myself. I couldn't trust Finn or Connor to watch her at my house. I have to take things into my own hands and I fuck them up. Maybe Brynn is right and I don't belong in the position I hold.

"This wasn't about the money, Declan." Ronan's rumble makes me tense. "It was about principle. She stole. They want her dead. She humiliated them, and we're protecting her—in fact, we are ensuring she will always be protected, and they will stop at nothing to make sure she dies before that wedding."

"The alliance, though..." Connor's comment comes on the back side of Ronan's obvious statement.

"The alliance won't go through without the wedding." I turn to the leader of our family, our chief, and I say, "I'm gonna hunt him down right now." Anger surges through me. I can barely control my urge to shatter this glass against my fireplace. "I'm gonna go out there and find him and slit him from pelvis to sternum."

"Now hold on," Ro says, pressing a hand to my chest. He sets his glass down and sucks in a deep, calming breath. But there's no breath deep enough to calm me. I'm outraged. The man attempted to kill my wife-to-be. "You're not thinking clearly. We have a plan."

"He shot up my car on the side of the road!" I scream, and my arms fly upward at the same time. I throw the glass into the hearth, and it shatters and sends splinters skittering across my wood floors. "She's my wife, Ro. We're not talking about an asset or a 'package'. She belongs to me, and he's threatening that."

I lean into his hand and he glares at me sternly. He knows I won't rebel against him, that my hands are tied and as long as he demands we hold off, I have to obey him. He knows that because of the situation I've put myself in, I would be openly telling this family that I hate him and his authority over me if I go against him in this, and he knows I won't do that.

But I want to.

My God, do I want to find Sebastian and use the tendons on his body to tie up every one of his enemies and burn them alive.

"Declan, take a breath. Control this." His eyes bear down on me, and I clench my jaw. His calculated stare is like my father's—dark, menacing, angry. I can't resist him or I'm risking my life. "The best thing we can do is go through with our plan. Your marriage is a death warrant to his desire. He won't lay a finger on her as long as she is your wife."

I'm seething, ready to tear Ronan's head off too, but I can't do anything about it. "Then bring the minister. I'll marry her now." My chest feels like it will explode. Protecting Isla is my number-one priority now, and it isn't even about this fucking alliance with her father anymore. It's her. I love her. I won't let anything happen to her.

"Breathe," he says again, "and take it slow. The publicity from the ceremony at my house is what we need. We want every head of every family in this city to know she belongs to us. That she's one of us now. The wedding at my home will go on as planned, and she will be safe."

He pulls away from me, and I watch Connor set his drink down. The expression on my younger brother's face is less certain, but even if he were to agree with me and want to hunt Sebastian down, we'd have to face Ronan's wrath.

I'm stuck. My hands are tied, and my brother is leaving.

"Do me a favor and make sure Maeve sleeps a little. She likes to helicopter over her patients." Ronan walks out, and Connor offers a look of compassion as he follows, and I'm stuck with my rage and my liquor, wishing I could murder that bastard for even thinking of hurting Isla. I won't let him get her, and I won't let anyone touch her ever again. Even if in the end, she still doesn't want me, I will protect her just like I promised.

14

ISLA

My head is pounding and the light nausea lingering is enough to keep me from resting despite feeling exhausted. That and the relentless nightmares I'm suffering. I'm alone in the room, still in Declan's giant bed. It smells like him, which is mildly pleasant. It's a subconscious trigger that lulls me into a sense of safety. Breathing him in during the middle of that attack was the only thing that kept me sane.

My entire body feels sore, the ache so deep it penetrates my bones. Much of the accident and the fire fight that followed are lost from my memory, but my body remembers. Every tender purple spot on my flesh tells the story of where I was struck or slammed against things. My knees feel raw as mince from being ground across the pavement. It hurts to bend my legs too.

I've been living in denial, and it's obvious now. My naivety is probably obvious to Declan and his brothers too. Had I been alone out there, no doubt I'd have been raped, tortured, and eventually killed by Sebastian O'Reilly and his men. They would surely have brought me to him so he could take his fill too, dishonoring me and humiliating me before dragging out my murder in a slow and agonizing fashion.

But I'm safe here thanks to Declan and his brothers. I'm in his warm bed, comfortable as I can be with all these bruises, and allowed to rest and recover at my pace. I'm not sure how many days it's been. I remember taking a few meals and throwing them up instantly. Maeve says it's the head injury, and I can't wait until that heals. I don't think I could escape now if I tried. My body is too weak, which means I have to plot out a new path forward and give myself time to recover fully.

It also means the time table I'm on is too short for an escape before this wedding. But I'm not as bothered by that as I was before. Even if I do say yes to the dress, I can still escape. My new identity won't be married. She'll be free to do as she pleases, and I will find love someday. Maybe not like him, definitely not like this family. But true love that's safe.

"How do you feel?" I hear, and I turn over to see Declan standing behind me. He's wearing only his towel around his waist, his body glistening with moisture. I never heard the shower running, though the loud ringing in my ears from the blow to my head is deafening. I may not hear soft sounds like that for a while.

"Sore," I croak, turning all the way around to face him. I lie on my side wondering why he looks at me so differently now, with softness and compassion. Where is the monster who murders people and enforces the O'Rourke law? For some reason, this version of him intimidates me, puts me under a spell that has me curling inward. This one is more dangerous than the other. This one will consume my heart and soul. The other can only kill my body.

"He's a dangerous man, Isla." Declan walks toward me, brushing a hand through his soggy locks. Water drips from his soggy strands and runs across his chest. The Celtic cross there suggests loyalty to his brothers and their criminal organization. His other tattoos aren't as meaningful, and I can admire how he stands by his brothers. But their sins are just too dark to overlook.

"You're a dangerous man." My words are hollow. I'm still numb. I don't really know if I believe that anymore, that Declan is a dangerous man—at least not to me. He's done nothing but try to convince me to let him protect me. He's not laid a hand on me except the times I asked for it. But I saw how he slaughtered those men—six of them in cold blood, lying on that pavement.

"They've already tried to kill you once. If they can't do that, they'll go after your family. And they've already tried that too." He stalks forward using the corner of the towel to dry his arm, and I jerk up in the bed.

My mind goes to my father and mother, to Rebecca. Sebastian is hunting down everything I hold dear, and all over a measly two hundred grand. His net worth is hundreds of millions. Why does he even care about it?

"I'll give it back," I say, standing up. The thin T-shirt I wear—one of Declan's he loaned me—and my panties are hardly enough to keep me warm or comfortable. I wrap my arms over my middle and look him in the eye. "I know right where it is. I can go dig it up and give it back. Please…" I want him to help me.

I'm under no illusion that he cares about me at all. This entire thing is just an arrangement to him. It doesn't matter that my edge toward him has started to soften or that I'm seeing things about him that I don't hate. It doesn't matter that he treats me nicely or protects me or that I feel the safest when I'm in his arms now—I have since that moment on the street when that blood from his shirt stained my palm.

I know I'm nothing more than a business transaction to him and he won't even stop to think about it if he has to put a bullet in my head. I'm a means to an end, but I have to plead with his human side, the side I see staring back at me right now. My family can't be harmed. It terrifies me.

"He doesn't care about the money," Declan says, walking toward his dresser. He lets the towel fall, his back to me. I see the scars there, ones I remember watching being sewn up and a few more I don't remember. But I've felt them under my fingertips when he had me, made me his.

"Then make him care," I snap, stalking over to him. His head hangs, and I stand by his side, glaring. "Go fecking find him and make him take it back." I'm heaving, trembling with the realization that I've put a bullseye on my family's backs. It probably comes across as anger, because despite what they say about me, I'm not a fucking banshee. I'm not going to break down crying.

"It doesn't work that way."

"Fecking make it work," I say, jabbing a finger into his chest. He's standing here naked in front of me, but I'm not even looking at the corded muscles on his ribs and abs or the fact that his dick is halfway stiff, probably from being around me while he's nude. I need answers, and I need comfort, and it's not easy for me to ask for it, especially from someone I should hate.

"I can't just snap my fingers, Isla," he says, and he looks up at me with a jade storm in his eyes. The hints of emerald are still flashing compassion, but I can see his temper roiling. If I anger him enough, maybe then he'll do something.

"So you'll let them take me? And what, rape me, slit my throat, murder my family? Do you think a marriage license will keep me safe?" My whole body is heaving now, shaking from fear and rage. My head throbs harder, and I feel like I might throw up, and when he opens his mouth to protest, it makes me snap.

"Mother of God, woman, you—"

I smack him hard, so hard his head pops to the left before his hand shoots up and grabs my wrist. He backs me against the wall and has both my arms pinned over my head before I can even protest, and his hot breath dances over my face.

"I tried to tell you, Isla, that the only way out of this is to trust me to protect you." He's strong, squared shoulders, chiseled muscles. My body floods with warmth as I imagine him pulling me against his chest to safety, not at all what my anger wants, but the fearful child inside me, the one terrified of losing her parents and only sibling, craves it.

"Screw off. I'm not marrying you," I blurt, but I know I will. I'll do anything to save them. This is all my doing. I can't live with that guilt.

"Why can't you just listen to me? How many more times do they have to come at you before you do?" He grits his teeth, and I turn my head away. I know he's right, and I hate it. They're coming like a devil in the night, and I don't have any choice but to submit to him.

"What are you going to do, fuck me into submission?" My words are harmless, a taunt flipped his way to incite his anger. Maybe then, he will unleash the beast I know too well, the one who consumes my doubts and reminds me of how powerful he is. Makes me feel safe.

"Do you want me to fuck you into submission?" His lips are dangerously close to my ear now, his cock hard and pressed on my bare thigh. He gets off on this too.

"I'm expecting nothing less."

Declan bites my earlobe but he doesn't release my hands. My body shudders as his other hand gropes my tit, squeezing and kneading it. I arch my back, silently begging for more. His hand travels down to the hem of my shirt, lifting it up and off in one fluid motion. I'm now naked except for my panties, but not for long. He hooks his fingers on the waistband and pulls them down, leaving me bare and exposed to his hungry eyes.

"Spread your legs," he growls as he releases my hands. I do as I'm told because defiance is no longer an option. He steps back, his erection still throbbing between his legs. "You're so wet." He smirks, running a finger through my folds and bringing it to my lips. "Taste yourself."

I taste myself on his finger, the musk of my arousal mixed with my shame. I close my eyes and suck his digit, moaning softly as he caresses my breast.

"That's it, baby." His voice is low, husky, and it sends shivers down my spine. He pushes two fingers inside me roughly, testing my entrance before he pulls out and brings them to my lips again. "Open your eyes. Look at me." I open my eyes reluctantly and meet his dark ones. "You want this, don't you?"

"Yes," I whimper. "I want you to possess me." There's something about it, the way he dominates me and makes me feel small. It feels safe, and I don't know why. Maybe because in my weakness, he's strong and I can trust that strength, or maybe it's something else. Maybe I'm falling for him.

Declan steps forward and pushes me against the wall, his erection pressing against my core. "Say it again, Isla. Tell me you want me to fuck you into submission. Tell me you want me to dominate you and force you to be my fuck toy."

"I—" I gasp as he enters me roughly, stretching me to the limit. "Ah, God!"

"Say it!" he growls, thrusting into me mercilessly.

"Yes... Make me your toy," I moan, my nails digging into his thighs. He's not gentle, but I don't want him to be. I want him to show me how much he needs this, how much he needs me. His hips smack against mine, each impact sending jolts of pleasure through my body. Then his hand comes down on the side of my ass in a hard crack that shakes me.

"Oh, God," I whimper, edging closer to orgasm, pushing my body against his in a desperate attempt to feel him deeper inside me.

"You like that, don't you?" he growls, smirking as he spanks me again, this time harder. "Tell me you like it."

"I... I like it," I moan, my body on fire as he pounds into me relentlessly. Pain and pleasure intertwine as one, the sting of his hand a delicious reminder of who has control here.

"Say it louder, Isla. Tell me how much you love it when I mark you as mine." It's humiliating and degrading, but he's right—I do love it. I love it so much, I keep coming back when I know my ultimate goal is to be far away from him, so far away from this life.

"I ... love it..." I pant, and an orgasm racks my body, making me jolt and convulse as he continues to fuck me against the wall. I'm trembling, weak in the knees as his scent curls around me and sucks me deeper into his vortex.

When he pulls out, I think I'm free, ready to curl up on the bed and resign myself to my fate, but he has other plans. Declan turns me around and forces my body to bend over his dresser. His dick prods at my backside as he grips my hair and pulls my head back at an odd angle.

"Feck, your ass is sexy..." His dick slides up and down my crack, smearing my moisture around.

"No, Declan... not there," I whimper, but it's too late. He's already inside me, stretching me in a way that burns like hellfire but feels so damn good. He pulls out and shoves his cock back in, harder this time, making me scream.

"Relax, Princess." He grits his teeth, and I clench around him. God, it feels so good, I can't breathe. "That's it, take Daddy's cock."

"Daddy?" I moan as he thrusts into me again and again.

"Yes, I'm your daddy now, and you're my little toy. Say it." His grip on my hair tightens, his thrusts harder and faster as he pounds into me relentlessly.

"I... I'm your little toy." My whimpers precede a second orgasm, this one more powerful than the first. And he seems to get off even more on it, feeling the pulsing of my tight hole around his thick girth. I feel like I'm tearing in two, but it's the most exquisite feeling I've had in my life.

How can I simultaneously hate everything this man stands for, everything I'm being forced to do for my family, and still find that I'm in love? How can I enjoy this when I hate it in principle and in deed?

I feel his release deep inside me and shudder as he lets go of my hair. I lie there draped over the end of the dresser as he pumps in and out of me a few more times then pulls out. It hurts, feels like I'm split open, but the relaxation comes in waves. I'm dizzy and weak. He helps me to bed and covers me.

When he presses a kiss to my forehead, he promises, "You'll see, Isla. I'll take care of you. You'll have everything you want and your family will be safe. Rest now, Princess..."

And my eyes shut with fatigue and afterglow. I don't have energy to fight right now. But I can dream of my escape and pray that when the time presents itself, I'll have the courage and the desire to run. Heaven help me if I fall any farther.

15

DECLAN

The rehearsal for our wedding was so different from most typical weddings. I'm sure it's left Isla feeling terrified. She's done nothing but cling to me the entire evening. If the speech Ronan gave about the security team didn't scare her, the trip through the weapons cache had to have. He's gone so far overboard to make sure none of Sebastian's creeps sneak in to harm her, and I'm glad. I just wish the look of panic in her eyes weren't so desperate.

"You okay?" I ask for the thousandth time. Isla nods, but her arms wrap around my bicep tightly. She's flushed with perspiration, but she shivers as she holds me. "You look as white as a ghost."

"I'm fine," she says tightly as I walk her out of the large tent Ronan had erected in his yard toward the house.

I'm not sure if it's still the fact that she's being forced into this against her will or if it's really fear. Or maybe it's just pre-wedding nerves. I have a few of my own, but mine aren't centered around the idea of giving up my bachelorhood. Mine stem from the idea that O'Reilly may try something and even the most prepared man can still be caught off guard.

"Time for dinner," Maeve says as she passes by our snail's pace. She touches Isla's arm lightly and smiles at us. With the wedding now only hours away, both Maeve and Ronan insist that we stay here tonight. They prepared a room for us against Isla's protest about the bride not seeing the groom before the wedding.

"Coming," I say, picking up my step. My brothers are all here, all prepared to stand as witnesses to this event that's supposed to be joyous and fulfilling. To this family, it will, but I'm afraid that Isla won't find it that. She'll run the first chance she gets, and maybe that's why Ronan has us stay here tonight. He's thinking the same thing. She wants out, not because she disdains her father or his well-being, but in spite of it, she still feels managed and controlled.

"Can I skip?" she asks, and the large saucer eyes she casts in my direction almost make me say yes to her, but my conscience is seared. My back is up against the wall.

"It will go smoothly, and then I can help you retire..." I keep the words tight and my tone firm, but I allow some remorse to creep out in my expression as I nod at her and gesture for her to enter the dining room first.

Her shoulders sag and she sits in an empty chair. I plant myself next to her and settle in. The chef has prepared a hearty meal of black pudding, Guinness stew, and boxty, and if I know my brother, there will be Bailey's cheesecake for dessert. My eyes devour the feast set out and make my mouth water and my stomach grumble.

One by one, my brothers file in, Ronan and Maeve seated near the head of the table. He offers the traditional Irish blessing and we dig in. I watch Isla begin to relax a little, sipping her wine and only nibbling at the food on her plate. She looks overly tired, and I'm about to suggest that we leave the table early so she can get to bed when Finn chimes in with a topic I wish I never had to hear again.

"So, D," he says cooly, using a childhood nickname reserved for conversation only when family is around, "I hear you have trouble stirring up..." Finn's dark eyes flick up to meet mine, and Ronan takes notice too. He sets his fork down and uses his napkin to wipe his mouth as I finish chewing my bite.

Isla's head hangs, but I can see the way she's so tense. I want to protect her from all of this family nonsense, but she has to get used to it at some point. We do family dinners a couple of times a month, and after tomorrow, she will be attending all of them.

"Yeah, well, we don't have to talk about it," I grumble, and I push the potatoes around on my plate with my fork.

"I think we do," Ronan says firmly, and he folds his hands over his plate and stares at me. I'm sick of being the subject of their conversations, especially over dinner. I wasn't the only one who spoke with our late cousin during his rebellion, but I'm the one who is being pinned to the mat and my life examined with a magnifying glass.

"Ro, please..." I shake my head and shove a potato in my mouth, and Isla looks up at me with curiosity. I hide the wince I want to let sneak out. I'll never live this down, my mistake. My family will hold this over my head for the rest of my life, and it's one of the reasons freedom from this entire organization has been so tempting to me.

"Your own choices brought you to this point, Declan. You can't make a mistake like that and then think you can walk away without consequences. They've lost faith in you." Ronan's eyes are as hard as steel, almost as black too.

"Feck's sake," I grunt. I'm sick of hearing his lectures.

"I'm just sayin', he's stirrin' up trouble." Finn's head dips as he wipes his mouth and drops his napkin onto his empty plate. "Ro's right, D. The family lost confidence in you. I'm worried they're gonna call for your head or at the very least, your dismissal."

My younger brother worries too much. There's no reason to believe my cousins and our trusted soldiers will openly call for me to be removed. I'm here proving myself now. If my willingness to cast the rest of my life into this family by way of arranged marriage doesn't show my loyalty to them, nothing ever will.

"I'll handle it," I grunt, and I touch Isla's knee under the table. I'm more than ready to leave now. I'd like to put distance between myself and my brothers, and I'm sure I will always feel like this every time they bring up my near failure.

"The fact that you entertained Eamon's snakish lies for even a second is all the doubt they need." Ronan continues his lecture, and my eyes meet Connor's. None of them know he actually made the plan to go, to flee, and was trying to convince me to go with him. I will keep that secret to my grave because to betray him would be to betray myself. Blood is thicker than water and Connor knows it. His ears burn bright red but he speaks up.

"Yeah, the family saw, so what? He's here now, doing the right thing." I nod at him, and his shoulders rise and fall in a calming sigh.

"You're right," Ro says, now with his eyes locked on me alone. Maeve looks tense next to him, shoulders squared, head hanging like Isla's. She's been part of these family meals where I've been reamed more than once. She knows how the lecture could escalate to screaming, but this time with my bride to be by my side, I will myself not to snap.

"Ronan, please..." I say again. I'm doing everything in my power to correct my stupid mistake and protect my brother from feeling the same heat. We were both foolish to think Eamon could ever have led this family. I was an idiot for entertaining the idea that Ronan wasn't the man for the job.

"This wedding will go a long way toward appeasing them, and until they fall in line and stand behind you, I told you to handle the problem." He tips his chin. "If you can't do that, maybe you aren't the enforcer I thought you were." His eyes narrow, and I stand up smoothly, nudging Isla to join me. She rises as I nod at my leader, my oldest brother, the chief, and huff out a sigh.

"We'll retire now so we'll get enough sleep for the wedding. See you all in the morning." And with that, I place my hand in the small of her back and let it ride there as I escort her to the room prepared for us. This wedding can't come soon enough. I'd have done it weeks ago if he let me. And when it's over, if Brynn keeps stirring up shit, I'm gonna bring the hammer down. The man won't know what hit him.

16

ISLA

Dinner was tense. As Declan shuts us into the room Ronan prepared for us to sleep in tonight, all I can think is how tense things are. The number of weapons this family has stashed on this property for something like a wedding is terrifying. Part of me believes it isn't safe to even go outdoors, let alone spend all day out there under a tent, signing my life away. And I don't want my parents here. Rebecca and Mum will be horrified to see the situation.

Da really got himself in deep this time. I wonder, as I walk into the bathroom to put on a silk nightgown, if my father actually knows the type of men he's handed me over to. If he knows they trade in blood and steel like this. If he knows the life I'll be sentenced to live out the rest of my days should I never be able to escape from their hands. A life of crime or a life on the run. Those are my options.

"I'm sorry," Declan says through the door as I drop my skirt and blouse on the bathroom countertop. My eyes catch my own reflection in the mirror, and I see the ugly yellow and green marks everywhere. The accident and the way those men hit me—it's healing but still painful.

"For?" I say back, not really sure what he means. If it's an apology for locking me away, forcing me to marry him, I'll accept it. Then I'll plead with him to help me get away. After everything that's happened, he surely has to see how scary this is for me. They burned my house to the ground. They ran us off the road and nearly killed me. He almost lost his life trying to protect me.

The O'Reillys are dangerous. They won't stop coming for me until I'm dead. I know men like the O'Rourkes have ways to help people vanish. They cover up crimes all the time. It would be simple.

"For dinner... for the whole day. For scaring you..." The door pushes open, and I stand there in nothing but my bra and panties, hands on the bra clasp.

It isn't the first time Declan has seen me like this, but his eyes this time don't flush with erotic desire like normal. This time, they sweep over my marred skin and his lips turn downward in a frown. I shake my head and sigh, turning away from him. I don't like him seeing me like this because it reminds me how much I want him, how good he makes me feel, how I long for his hands to bring me to that precipice and then pull me back in.

And if I think of those things, I forget how scary this whole family is. How they murder and steal and cover it up. How they've got something over my father to the point where he can't even get away from them without trading my life.

It isn't fair. It isn't right. And I have to focus on that as Declan's hands gently touch my biceps and he presses a kiss to the back of my shoulder.

"I promise it won't always be like this. We'll get through the wedding and you'll see. Life can be very normal." His words tighten my gut, make it roil with confusion and indecision. I want to believe him, but I don't. How could I ever settle into this life with him to the point where murder and thievery became normal?

"Help me," I say softly, almost so quietly, I can't hear myself. I don't know if he hears me, but my heart thuds against my chest in anxiety that he does hear me. It's fear of being punished for how I feel—the way Ronan breathes down Declan's neck for almost defecting. And it's fear of being rejected—being told he can't or won't help me. Maybe even a little fear that he will help me and that I'll never see him again.

"I can't, Isla," he whispers. As he does, he turns me to face him, and I rest my hands on his chest. I wish I had some way to take my raw emotion out of my chest and give it to him so he could sense what I'm feeling, the dread and panic. So he could see how desperately I need his help.

"You could get me a new name, a new identity for me and my family. I could go where Sebastian's men can't find any of us, to Russia or the United States. Please…" I realize I'm begging, how weak I sound. But I'm only doing it because I know he cares. On some level, he knows my heart. Why else would he truly protect me like this? Why would he offer me any compassion or sympathy, any gentleness?

"I could, but it wouldn't be right." His eyes cloud with frustration. There's a lot on the line for him too. I know that. If I don't marry him, what will happen to his family? I heard what Ronan said at dinner. I just don't know what it all means.

Those questions won't go away. They swirl around between us, and I feel compelled to ask him because I see in his eyes the desperation for relief, the way I feel. If I can make him feel relief, I know he will want me to feel it too. He'll help me.

"What was that about? What did you do?" I ask, thinking about dinner and how his brothers spoke to him. Connor seemed to be the only one defending him.

"We're not so different, Isla…" He brushes the pad of his thumb over my bottom lip and cups my cheek. "I almost ran away too, and now I have to prove my loyalty to this family. I just wish I could help you see what I see now. How Ronan helped me open my eyes to the wealth this family offers, and I'm not talking about money."

My heart sinks ever so slightly, but I believe him. I do believe there is a richness in this family that I could tap into. I see it in the way they respect each other, support each other. I see the way Maeve treats them, and given what I know about her, I can't see why such a respectable doctor like her would allow her life to be linked to this.

I know Declan feels that pull because it's the same pull I feel toward my family and being loyal to them. It's why I will actually walk down that aisle to become his wife if it gets my Da out of hot water, but the first instant I have to get out of here, I'll take it. Maybe while everyone is distracted at the wedding. I just can't stay here. I can't allow them to rule over me when I haven't even been given the choice to submit. My choice was stolen from me.

"You'll see," he says, pulling me against his chest. "I promise."

I do feel safe with him. I feel wanted and comforted in his arms. Maybe it was our joint near-death experience, the accident, or the way he responded afterward by bringing me into his bed, but I do trust him that much. It's that affection that warms me from the inside out. If I run tomorrow, that means tonight is the last night I get with him. Even if I have to disappear now and come back to my family later, I know I have to go, which means a goodbye.

"D," I say, mimicking the way Finn spoke so vulnerably by using a nickname.

Declan's eyes turn down to meet mine as he gives me a bit of space. "Yeah," he says, narrowing his eyes in confusion. I'm sure the nickname probably feels odd coming from me.

"What would you do if I were a really, really bad girl?" I bite my lip and bat my eyelashes, and at first, his gaze storms. Like lightning bolts behind his irises, I see the lights flick on, recognition dawning on him.

"How bad?" he asks, and his hand rests on my hip, strumming the elastic of my panties.

"Very, very bad... I think so bad, you'd have to hunt me down and punish me." Warmth spreads through my body as I reach up and undo my bra clasp and let it fall. "What would you do to me?"

Finally, the point hits its mark. Declan hooks a finger through the elastic of my panties and tips his chin up. "Well," he says, reaching up with his other hand to remove his tie, "I'd have to punish you for sure. You'd probably need to be tied up so you don't run again." In a split second, his hands lash the tie around my wrists, and it makes a wave of lust shoot to my core.

It's bittersweet as he leads me into the bedroom. I've never felt so alive sexually as when he's dominating me. I'll miss it, so I pour every ounce of desire I have into it as he pushes me onto the bed and I get on all fours.

"You'd better catch me. I'm gonna run away," I say, shaking my ass.

Declan's hand comes down on my ass hard, smacking me and leaving a fiery red handprint. "You'll see how I catch my prey, Isla," he growls, and it sends chills down my spine.

I wait for him as he undresses. My hands throb from the tie wrapped so tightly around my wrists. My body is exposed, chilly in the air-conditioned room, but I don't move a muscle. I can feel his eyes devouring me, probably zeroing in on the dot of moisture soaking through my panties, showing my desire for him.

"You're a dangerous woman, Isla," he growls, unbuckling his belt and letting his pants drop to the floor. He growls low in the back of his throat and strides over to me. His cock is hard, straining against the fabric of his underwear, and it makes something inside me grow hotter and wetter, knowing I have that much power over him. I do that to him and I don't have to try, much the same way that he makes me ache to be filled just by being near me.

He shoves his boxers down and his cock springs free, and I moan at the sight of it. Thick and veiny, it's the most beautiful thing I've ever seen. "I know. Now punish me," I tell him, praying if there is a God in heaven, he'll ignite a fire in my core that will detonate the deepest pleasure I've ever known.

His hand comes down on my ass again, harder this time. I yelp but I don't back down. It doesn't deter me. It only makes me want him more, to feel his hands on every curve of my body. The stinging pain mixes with desire, and the swirling emotions in my belly coalesce into one. Need.

"I'll show you punishment," he grunts. His hands tear the silky, moist fabric of my panties down to my knees, and he leaves them there, prohibiting me from spreading my legs. Then Declan's fingers shove into me from behind, searching my pussy with force, making me gasp, drawing pants of pleasure as he fucks me with them. He doesn't go slow. He doesn't try to ease himself in. He simply impales me with swift thrusts that make my eyes water with the combined pleasure-pain.

I want to reach for my clit, rub myself, aid in the stimulation, but my hands are tied. I buck into him, backing up as he finger fucks me, whimpering for more. The delicious friction is eased only by the moisture my body makes, and his thick digits draw unholy gasps from my throat.

"I'm bad... please, punish me," I plead, not even sure what I'm saying anymore. This game isn't me, but how else do I ask him for what my body craves knowing full well that I'm going to run away tomorrow? To be soft is to let my heart be vulnerable. I remind myself that this is sex and nothing more, and after this, I'll remind myself again that leaving is what's best. "Please," I whimper.

Declan growls again, this time a low, rumbling growl that makes me tremble with anticipation. He withdraws his fingers, and I whine my

THE ENFORCER'S REDEMPTION

disapproval, but he only reaches for the drawer of the nightstand, grabbing something cold and metallic that clinks together.

"You're a very bad girl, Isla," he growls, and I can hear the lust in his voice. He drags whatever it is he's picked up along my spine, sending shivers down my spine. The surface is smooth, but the edges are hard. "But I think I know just how to punish you."

The cold object chills my entrance before he shoves it into my pussy, and a symphony of pain and pleasure that melds together until I can't tell the difference anymore follows. I'm whimpering, feeling the cold object fucking me, his hand gripping my ass and squeezing it. It's hard and thick, striking my back wall with its full depth, and I'm on the edge, ready to come apart when he rips it out of me. I shudder and whimper at the sudden lack of anything inside me.

"Oh, God... shit," I grunt, panting for breath as he replaces whatever it was with his cock. The contrast from cold to hot is exquisite, and I'm ready to snap. "I'm so close," I tell him, and he begins pumping into me. His full girth and length are as large and deep as whatever toy he just used on me, but the heat is exquisite now following the chill.

I clench my teeth, clamp my eyes shut, and then I'm shattering, my back arching as my orgasm rocks through me, shaking me to my very core. Declan groans behind me, sliding his cock into my soaking pussy that is already dripping with juices. He pounds into me like a man possessed, growling and surging inside me. Every delicious thrust of his hips pushes me farther into the depths of pleasure. I claw at the sheets until I fall over and the waves begin to subside.

My world spins. I see stars, and I see the flashlight on the bed next to me, soaked in my juices. Its long, metallic blue handle is coated from being inside me, and I can't even take a moment to think as Declan spreads my thighs, pins my knees to my shoulders, and pushes into me again from this angle. He's large and dominant, tossing me like a rag doll, and his cock hits my cervix with so much force, I whimper.

"Shit!" I hiss. I use the restraint around my wrists to hook around his head and pull him down for a kiss, almost crushing myself in the process. I can barely breathe, but the sensations are otherworldly.

The room is spinning, and then he's kissing my neck, biting me hard enough to draw blood. I cry out in ecstasy-pain as he sucks on the wound he's just made, his cock still pounding me into the mattress. His rhythm is relentless until I can take no more, and I come again, this time with a scream that reverberates off the high ceilings. Declan growls, his cock twitching inside me as he orgasms too, spilling his hot seed into me.

We collapse in a heap, my back pressed against his chest, legs tangled together like vines. I don't have the strength to move, and neither does he, judging by his labored breathing in my ear. "That was…" I trail off, unable to find the words to describe what just happened between us.

He reaches around and unties the tie from my wrists then holds me. I lie in his arms catching my breath, rehearsing my mantra… I'm a free woman. I'll be free tomorrow. They can't make me stay. My stomach rolls again, the way it has been doing for days. Nerves. The anxiety of it all, of running from these powerful men and praying I don't get killed in the process, is killing me. I can't eat. I can't sleep.

And tomorrow is the day.

When they're all distracted, I'll run.

And God be with me. Because if I do, there's no turning back.

17

DECLAN

Isla lies peacefully on the bed, sleeping. My handprint on her ass will leave a bruise, but it's one she'll treasure, unlike the others that are now fading. The ones on her face are mostly healed, but Maeve and the wedding planner will have to help her cover them for our ceremony this afternoon. I dress quietly then press a kiss to her temple before slipping out.

The way she taunted me last night, the Sub-Dom act, was erotic. Isla is finally coming around, and I think maybe she's going to end up just fine. I knew when Sebastian's men attacked us on the side of the road, something shifted. She softened at that point, clung to me. She welcomed my attention and presence after that, and last night, the way she initiated sex immediately after I told her this was the way it had to be... I know today will be fine, as far as she's concerned.

It's the rest of the day I'm worried about.

I tighten my tie, make sure my suit jacket is buttoned up correctly, and make my way down to the living room. The scents of bacon and coffee float around in the air, but I'm not hungry, and given my druthers, I'd take a shot of those Writer's Tears over the black roast

Ro's maid cooked up. I need to calm my nervous system and stay focused.

I pass the den where everything inside is layered with pinks, whites, and satin. Maeve and the woman she hired to help with the plans—a leggy mare with bright platinum hair—hold up a dress, ogling it. Maeve sees me, and I nod at her.

"Treat her like a princess today, Ladies. You know she deserves it." I wink at Maeve, who snickers.

"I can't wait! She's going to be a beautiful bride," Maeve calls, and I move away from the door. No doubt, my beautiful bride-to-be will put all others to shame. I'm confident in that. She outshines the sun when she smiles, no wedding gown or fancy hair needed.

Pressing on, I walk to the living room where I hear men's voices. Ronan and Finn are there talking. I recognize the din of their chuckles and the lightheartedness in their tones. It's a day for celebration for them—binding the two families together. I wish there were another way that didn't make Isla feel imprisoned, but our fathers wanted it this way. Mick wants it this way. It's been the plan for twenty years now, though everyone thought maybe Connor would be the lucky goat.

"Good morning," I grunt as I strut in and head straight for the alcohol. They lounge on the sofa casually, coffee mugs in hand. Neither of them is dressed for the day yet, and while we still have hours, I find that frustrating. There are so many things to go over before our guests start to arrive. We'll have the press, members of parliament, and the place has to be on lockdown too. So much to do.

"Never pegged you for the nervous groom." Finn laughs, and I scowl as I fill a tumbler with whiskey, at least four shots. I down them in a few gulps and wipe my mouth with the back of my hand.

"Joke all you will, but this isn't just a marriage. This is an alliance between two very powerful forces." Just the thought of it makes the dark cloud of anger, gloom, and apprehension float over my head.

"Come... Sit." Ronan nods at the armchair opposite him, and I glower at his dark blue toweling robe, the plaid flannel pajama pants, and his white T-shirt. He never lets anyone see him like this but his brothers. It cheapens the austere façade he normally keeps and reminds me of our childhood, waking up on Saturdays to pancakes and eggs and shooting lessons in the garden with our Da.

I sit across from him, and he shoves the cup of black tar-like Greek coffee in my hand. "Drink," he orders, and I sigh. What would I do without my brothers to anchor me? I'm supposed to be relaxing and reveling in my impending union with a very beautiful woman, and all I can think of is what might go wrong. But so many things could. I can't get my mind to settle. My gut says something bad is on the horizon.

My brother's expression grows dark, and I tense as I sip from his cup. The sludgy richness of the coffee threatens to keep me awake for the next four months with just a sniff, and the first sip is as bitter as the throne of hell. But I drink it down and he pats me on the knee.

"You need to hear this from me, and before you freak the feck out, just listen." I stiffen again as I glance at Finn, whose head is hanging. I start to wonder why Connor and Lochlan aren't here. They were here last night. We were all at dinner, here for the walkthrough of the security for the ceremony. They should be here now, walking me through my last morning as a free man.

Then I realize the gut feeling I have isn't for something that might happen in the future. It's something that's already happened. I can see it in Ronan's eyes as he meets my gaze.

"What is it?" I ask as I set the mug on the coffee table and rest my hands on my knees.

"He struck while we slept, Declan." Finn's tone is tense, fraught with anger and malice. My eyes shift to Ronan as he speaks.

"Sebastian's men burned your home to the ground last night. There isn't a shred of anything left." He says it so casually, as if it shouldn't affect me, but rage instantly boils in my blood. I shoot to my feet and stare at him, not believing but yet at the same time fully trusting my brother. He knew. Somehow, Ronan knew there would be trouble on this, the eve of our wedding. It's why he brought us here, where we'd be safe. We could've been killed, either in the fire or as we fled the burning building.

"It's gone?" I breathe, feeling my throat constrict thinking that Isla could've died. How much longer will I have to fight these sick bastards?

"Gone," Ro says, standing. He rests a hand on my shoulder and nods at me. "We're almost there, Declan. We stay the course. They won't stop this wedding from taking place." He is adamant that this alliance happen, the marriage, the signing of a binding contract between families. I'm just trying to survive and keep my wife safe, the woman I love.

My mind shoots to Mick and Brennan, poor Rebecca. My eyebrows rise, and as if reading my mind, Ronan says, "The O'Connors suffered another attack too. They're safe, but their main barn is destroyed." Their main barn. The weapons cache…

"Rebecca?" I ask, fearing how Isla may react to hearing this news.

"All of them. They're safe. There was a fire fight, but they're sleeping peacefully. They've already told Rebecca everything." Finn's comment stings. Going into this without Isla understanding the fullness of what's at stake isn't right. I should tell her, but I'm bound by an oath, the way Mick wanted it. His own bloody shame over his life and the choices he made sickens me. But I know he believes women are soft, that they should be sheltered. Men are different, and had he any sons, this would play out very differently.

"Go to her," Ro says. "Make sure she's in good spirits. Let's make this day profitable for us all, and after that, we'll deal with the fallout."

He slaps me on the back and nudges me toward the door, and I'm the one left feeling gutted. With something so momentous, you'd think they'd want everyone involved to understand, but not this time. Not this secret. The precious cargo, my princess, she's the key to it all, and if I can't hold my shit together and keep her from running, it all falls apart.

Which means no one—absolutely no one—can tell her the truth. Not until that ring is on her finger.

18

ISLA

My palms are sweaty as I pull the overly garish dress up. Maeve stands behind me, working fastidiously to lash me into the thing. My eyes lock on to my reflection in the full-length mirror. I look tired, but the makeup covers the bruises well. And even though I'd have preferred a much simpler dress if this were my dream wedding, I can't say I hate the white satin cloaking me.

"Oh, gosh, it fits perfectly!" Maeve is more excited for this than is natural, but maybe she has no sister or something. I fully expect that if Rebecca were in this room, she'd be bubbling around this room all giddy and gushing over the romance of it all too.

"Yes," I say stiffly, smoothing my hands down my sides. The form-fitting bodice accentuates my full chest, which seems even larger with the cut of the fabric. I press the tops of my breasts, wishing they would stay in the fucking dress better. I'm not the most modest woman in the world and at times I wear a skimpy dress, but this thing puts my cleavage on display like no other.

"Oh, Declan is such a lucky man, Isla." Maeve primps my hair, fussing with it as she determines how best to pin the veil over my face. It's crusted in gems—diamonds and crystals—heavy, not something I'd have chosen for myself either.

My family isn't so well off, though we never lacked. Da provides the best for us, and even after I moved out on my own, he still managed to bring me gifts and spoil me. But they still live a modest lifestyle at the farm, unlike Declan's family, who like to flaunt their wealth. My wedding day should be simplicity and modesty, not thousand-dollar hair clips and a dress that cost more than my car.

"Is he?" I ask numbly, knowing what my plan is for the day, anyway. He's a tomb—sealed up emotions, brick walls behind which he hides. If he has any concern for me, he can't express it outside of demanding that I let him protect me.

Last night was incredible, the sex, anyway. But I am not allowing myself to naively follow the prodding of duty just because the sex is good. He's a good man. I can see that. But even that wouldn't keep me here. I deserve a chance to find a man who loves me deeply and passionately, someone who has all the best traits Declan possesses and at the same time allows me the freedom to make my own choices.

"Oh, every bride feels like this on her wedding day. I'm sure you'll be coaching me through it come August when Ronan and I take the walk down the aisle." Her smile in the reflection as she places my veil on my head is soft and warm. Whoever schooled her on this event left out huge details. I'm about to turn and explain how I'm being forced to wed in an arranged marriage I highly disdain when the door swings open.

Finn stands in the entrance wearing a striking black tuxedo, gesturing into the room. I see the gun on his hip and shudder. I want to scream and rant about how a wedding is no place for guns and violence, but it would do no good. I'm a trophy being awarded to a family of killers because my father owes a debt he can't pay. My head hangs briefly before I hear my mother's sigh.

I raise my head and see the tears in her eyes as she steps into the room, palms pressed together under her chin in a gesture of prayer. She's smiling, dressed in a beautiful purple dress suit with her hair twirled up in a French twist. And it's surprising to see her dripping in diamonds too—as if they're part of an unwritten dress code for a million-dollar wedding.

"I'll give you two privacy and see what the guys are up to." Maeve squeezes my arm before dashing out the door. Finn flicks a glance at me, and I notice his eyes ogle me for a second before he walks out and shuts the door and Mum rushes over to take my hands.

"Oh, Isla, you're so beautiful. This gown is so lovely." I can't tell whether she's happy or sad. I turn away, staring at myself in the mirror and willing my eyes not to leak the emotion I'm feeling.

"It's overdone, pretentious, gaudy." I don't hate it, but it will make running harder. At least the train is removable.

Mum sighs again, letting go of my hand to dab at her eyes with her fingers. She can't stop the tears from coming, and seeing her break down pulls my heartstrings. I'm normally put-together. I don't cry. I don't show weakness. It's the way Da taught both me and Rebecca, maybe because Mum cries enough for the rest of us. Life is hard, and it will kick you in the teeth and you have to be tough. I have to be tough.

"It's not as bad as you think it will be, Isla." She stands behind me where I can see her reflection in the mirror over my shoulder. She's not even trying to stop the tears now, but she does mask her true emotion behind a very plastic smile. She wants me to be brave, but seeing how she really feels makes the tears spring to my eyes, threatening to ruin the masterpiece Maeve made of my face.

"That's not true and you know it. I'm only doing this because I have no other choice." I turn, taking her hands now, letting my eyes flood my cheeks and drip to my chest below. The rivulets form a stream between my breasts and I shudder. "Help me. Find a way to get me out of this place. I'll disappear for a while and then send you instructions on how to meet me. I know we can get away, Mum—"

"Isla," she coos, patting my hand, "it's okay. Arranged marriages aren't as bad as you think they are. Declan is a good man." Her face is taut and drawn. This close to her, I can see the worry and sleep lines on her face. She's exhausted and she's not making sense.

I shake my head and start to protest, but what can I even say? My own mother is siding with them, pushing me into this life. "I don't understand. Why? Why me? Why can't you help me?"

The door swings open before a million other questions are able to come out. What did she mean by that? How does she know arranged marriages aren't awful? Was she pushed on my father the way I'm being pushed toward Declan? Can't anyone save me from this?

"They're ready," Maeve says gently, and I swipe at my eyes, shrinking back. I'm frigid suddenly, ready to vomit and shivering. The room seems to spin as Mum takes my hand and leads me to the door.

Da is there, elbow poised to usher me to my doom. The dress drags along behind me, and Maeve holds a massive pillowing bouquet of roses and vining white flowers that dangle down the front of my dress. I take it with shaking hands and grit my teeth, willing myself not to cry anymore.

"You look radiant, darling," Da says, but I can't even look at him. I can't blame him. Men make mistakes. Whatever his was, it's costing me, but I can see the pain in his eyes. It's costing him too.

Maeve takes the train of my dress and helps me out of the room toward the back door where we descend the patio stairs and walk toward the tent. I'm numb and hollow, a zombie walking through the grass, my pointy heels sinking into the moist earth.

"Da, please," I mumble softly when Mum moves ahead into the tent. I see Connor escorting her, then the large arch of roses near the front, beneath which Declan stands looking attractive as ever in his black tux.

"For the family, Isla." Da pats my hand and begins to escort me between the rows of chairs, and I, the silent, obedient daughter, go with him, thinking how at the first chance, I'm gone. I'll tear this train off and run, and they'll never find me.

I just have to make it through this ceremony.

19

DECLAN

She's a vision. Transformed by the skillful hands of Maeve and the wedding planner, Isla is a thing of beauty. The dress suits her, stealing my watchful eye. From my vantage point on the dais, I should be surveying the crowd, watching for threats, but I can't help myself from stealing a long, languid glance over her.

The dress fits her perfectly, pushes those thick, fleshy globes upward to almost inappropriate heights. Jealousy flares to life in my chest as I think of all the sick fucks in this tent, seated in the cushioned folding chairs, watching my beloved, beautiful bride as she passes. How their eyes must see what I see.

Movement near the back of the tent causes me to glance up and take notice. It's just Connor taking his position there after escorting Mrs. O'Connor to her spot near the front. I'm on edge. Everything threatens to trigger me. Under my left arm is my chest holster. I squeeze my bicep to my ribs as Isla nears, reminding myself that the weapon is there if I need it.

I'm not foolish enough to believe that Sebastian will honestly respect the silent rule, but the idea of Isla having my name as an added layer

ARIANA COOPER

of protection makes me want to get this over with even faster. She has no clue why it's so important, and the minute she's my wife, I no longer have to respect their ridiculous rules about keeping things a secret.

She doesn't look calm, though. As she rises onto the dais and stands facing me, she trembles. Her hands shake, jostling the petals on the flowers in her hands until Maeve takes it and stands behind her. Finn stands behind me, Mick near the stairs. He nods at us as the priest begins.

"Who gives this woman to be this man's lawful wife?" the priest asks, and Mick nods.

"Aye, her mother and myself," he says, bowing from the shoulders. His smile is forced but in a professional way. Mick and I have an understanding about this arrangement, and he knows how I feel. I had a talk with him this morning, letting him know that Isla is my precious treasure, title or not. I will do anything to cherish her and protect her and to honor the bonds of this marriage as if it were forged in the truest of loves. She's stolen my heart and she doesn't even know it.

"I..." Isla whimpers. "I can't..." she blurts out, and then she darts off the dais. Two, then three steps, stumbling down the stairs toward the rows of chairs where Ronan brandishes his weapon, resting it on his lap. Isla stops dead in her tracks, and I watch her eyes skim over the crowd of people.

Brennan cries, Rebecca beside her clinging to her mother. Our guests seem startled and shocked. Only a few of them know the truth of this arrangement—the mayor, who seems annoyed that Isla is hesitant, and the inspector general, who has the same disgruntled expression. A quiet murmur rises among the rest as Mick gently turns Isla back to the dais and Maeve straightens her train out as she ascends the stairs again.

"She's just a little nervous," Maeve says in a hushed tone. A few chuckles rise up as we all take our places again, but I see the terror in Isla's eyes. I wish I could change this.

I want to wrap my arm around her and shoot my way out of this tent, scoop her up and run away. That fear that paralyzes her is wrong and it should never happen. She should be free to make this choice on her own. We both should be. But there's no way out but through. I take her trembling hand and brush the pad of my thumb over her knuckles as the priest continues.

He reads a passage from the Bible, then a poem. His prayer is rousing, drawing grunts of approval from many of our guests, and when we exchange vows, Isla's voice is so meek no one can hear her but me and the priest. It's done. It's good enough. She is my wife, my partner, and now my property to protect.

I don't even wait for him to announce us or to tell me to kiss my bride. I pull her against my body and cup her cheek. My mouth covers hers, moving against her with hunger and desire. Isla is at first startled but soon relaxes into the kiss and melts into me, clinging to me as chuckles rise from the guests.

"I suppose you may kiss your bride," jokes the priest, and more roaring laughter ensues, but I continue kissing her until she's putty in my hands.

When I pull away, to the applause of the crowd as the priest pronounces us man and wife, I rest my forehead against hers. And as the music begins to play, I whisper, "It's done, Isla, and I'm never going to let anyone touch a hair on your head now. Do you understand? I will kill anyone who even looks at you."

I see her red-rimmed eyes and know she's been crying. At some point today, my beautiful bride has shed tears. I've never seen her cry, not even in the most frustrating or terrifying times. It worries me, and I want to ask, but she nods and the priest nudges my shoulder.

There will be time to investigate her feelings later, when this feast is over and the press have their fill of images to plaster all over the internet and every newspaper in the country. It isn't every day that an O'Rourke has a wedding, so this is huge news. Ronan is right. It's the fastest way to spread the word officially that Isla O'Connor is now an O'Rourke and thus off limits to our foes. It will put Sebastian in a very dangerous position if he continues his pursuit of her. Every family in this city will know it, and he'll make enemies of them all.

"Congratulations," Ronan says stiffly as he approaches. His eyes are raking over the crowd as people rise and start to meander toward us. My gut is torn up, knotted and roiling. It doesn't feel right. It feels like chaos. These are our vetted guests, already disarmed and personally hand-selected by Ronan to attend, in order to make the biggest impact and send the loudest message to Sebastian and the city at large.

"It doesn't feel right," I tell him under my breath. "Something feels wrong." Isla clings to my side still, though Maeve is here trying to get her to take the flowers. My heart is pounding, hairs on my arms standing on end. I should feel safe here to relax and celebrate, but I can't. I have a horrible feeling something is going to happen.

Lochlan is one of the first to greet me after Ronan, who stands stoically with me, scanning the crowd. "What is it?" Loch asks, and I shake my head.

"Something isn't right," I tell them both. "Loch, watch her. Keep her here by the fountain and don't let her out of your sight. Ro, we need to check the gate. I just have a bad feeling." Peeling Isla's arms from around my waist, I press a kiss to her temple. "Stay with him, alright? I'll be right back."

Isla nods at me, biting her lip. Her father approaches her, and I know here in the middle of this crowd, with her father and my brother watching her, Isla will be safe. Ro and I walk away, weaving under the tent between men who are setting up tables, rearranging the rows of chairs around them to transform the ceremony into the wedding feast. I have to check the gate and make sure Sebastian O'Reilly isn't around here.

"We've double checked all of the security in the last hour, Declan. This strange obsession that something will go wrong today is all in your head." Ronan is only humoring me because he understands the weight of what just transpired. We all understand it and soon, the whole city will be transformed by it.

"We can't be too safe. You know once things start rolling out in the city, we'll make new enemies." The "new enemies" we make aren't my concern. Somewhere along the line, this became less about defending my own honor and more about safeguarding the only thing in this life that makes it worth staying. If Isla is here, I can stick it out. We can have a good life together, and maybe one day, if she's still adamant that it has to be this way, we can find a path on our own in a safe way.

"Fair enough," he says, "but even without the O'Connor girl, we have what we need now." Ronan's callous statement enrages me. I almost snap and strike him, but I control myself, choosing to stand in his path and not allow him to move forward as I stare him down.

"She's not just a pawn, Ronan, and I'm sick of your treating this like a business transaction." Ronan's gaze steels, his eyes darkening to almost black. "She is my wife and I love her. Do you understand? Do not speak of her like an object again." I step forward, pressing my chest to his, and finally, I feel the relief I've been needing.

The nagging feeling of something going wrong lifts for a moment and I realize maybe it really is in my head. Ronan's lips purse, his eyebrows creeping closer to one another. He's not happy with my telling him off, but he respects me. I know he'd do the same if I spoke about Maeve that way.

"Fair enough," he says, "so prove it to this family then that your loyalty is to us. See this through while protecting her. It doesn't matter to me whether she is safe, but I can see how you feel about it." He pauses and huffs a sigh out his nostrils. "Our empire has just doubled in size, and more than ever, we'll depend on you. Get your head in the game, Declan. You can't be stuffing up because you caught feelings for her. Get that part straight."

I nod as my chest tightens. At last, my brother is finally letting go of his grudge. "As long as this family is behind me every step of the way, this new alliance will work. And nothing will stop us." My throat squeezes as I think of Isla alone on our wedding day, surrounded by that chaos. She needs me to anchor her or she'll be too frightened and maybe try to run again. "We should get back."

"Sure you don't want to check the gate again?" Ro asks, quirking an eyebrow as he smirks.

"Screw you," I say, pushing him playfully. He slaps a hand to the back of my neck and squeezes it as we start to walk back toward the chaos in his back yard. It feels as if a thousand pounds have been lifted off my shoulders now, and it's not just because I'm finally redeeming myself. It's because I feel like things are working out.

We enter the back yard where the entire place has been transformed. Tables are set. Guests are seated. The meal is being carried out by the staff, and Lochlan stands with Finn near the fountain in the center of the yard, but I don't see Isla. It makes my heart stop instantly and my blood runs cold.

Where is my wife? And why is my brother laughing as if it's the funniest day of his life? Who am I going to have to kill?

20

ISLA

When Declan walks away, following his "gut" about some supposed threat, I know it's my window. I thought he would never let me out of his sight today, but I'm being handed a golden opportunity straight from the hand of God. I watch him and Ronan vanish around the corner of the house as swaths of people funnel in and out of the house carrying table linens, centerpieces, and place settings.

Our guests mill about too, some of them nodding their congratulations and others chatting happily. Da offers a hug, Mum a few tears, and then a man named Aiden, whom I'm told works for Ronan, escorts them to a table near the far end of the tent where the string quartet is set up.

Lochlan isn't paying attention to me, chatting with a few men I've never met, but the moment I start to walk away, he nabs me, grabbing my arm tightly. "Where do you think you're going?" He grumbles, and I keep a plastic smile etched into my face. I've been emotional all day. I could use the nausea trick to get out of this, but despite having felt nauseous for a few weeks now over the stress of all of this, I'm not actually feeling sick right now.

"I have to pee, and I have a splitting headache. I was just going in to get out of the sun for a moment." I nod at the house, and he scowls at me. For a second, I think my window just closed, but when one door closes, heaven opens another, right? Maeve saunters over with a look of concern, and I grasp onto that instantly.

I may not be able to overpower a grown man with a gun, but this sweet little surgeon won't know what hit her.

"What's wrong?" she asks, her eyes bouncing between Lochlan's and mine. He looks like I've just committed a crime, but Maeve's innocence is her downfall. I bat my eyelashes and rub my temples, playing on my earlier hesitancy for this wedding. She's so naive about things, so gullible. She thinks what I'm going through is just wedding jitters.

"I have a horrible headache and I'm feeling parched. The ladies' room…" I raise my eyebrows, and she scowls at Lochlan.

"I'll take her, you ogre." Maeve hooks her arm around mine, and Loch stands in our way.

"Declan said not to let her out of my sight." He touches the butt of his gun, and Maeve rolls her eyes hard.

"They're married now, fool. Move out of my way or I'll inform Ronan you have zero hospitality when it comes to your new sister-in-law." With one hand planted on her hip, her head cocked at an accusing angle, Maeve stands her ground. Her authority in this family isn't lost on me. Lochlan looks hesitant, but he backs away and nods.

Maeve's perfume wraps around me in a comforting embrace as she guides me between the streams of people ushering in the party in my honor. I feign needing her, keeping with the act of having wedding jitters, and she starts to ramble.

"You'd think the men in this family would have a bit more compassion for all their ranting about how they treat wives." She sighs and pats my arm. "I'm sorry he's a pain in the ass, and I'm sorry you've a headache. Must be dehydration… Or more of those wedding nerves.

But the hard part is over now." She beams at me again as we enter the house. I don't know it as well as I know Declan's house, but I know the way to the front door. And I know that dragging this train down the street will be a nightmare. It'll slow me down too much.

"I think I spent too much time overthinking things," I tell her, and I have no trouble being honest about that. I've done nothing but overthink every step I've taken since the moment they showed up at my home and wrested me away from it.

"So you're feeling better?" she asks, gesturing toward the short hall leading to the toilets.

I nod and smile, and this time, it's a very genuine smile. I can see the light at the end of the tunnel—literally. The door to the side entrance past the garden and out to the street outside the gate is within view. I don't see anyone moving out there, and I'm almost home free.

"I do. I think you were right about wedding jitters. I pray you don't have the same nervousness I had the past few days over your wedding. I feel like it's made me a mess. I want to freshen up and... Oh—" I touch my fingers to my lips in another feigned action. I have to get rid of her, and I know just how to do it.

"Oh?" she says, tilting her head again. I find it comical. She's like a well-trained dog, heeding every command I give her. I feel bad in one respect. When Ronan finds out it was his very partner who led me away from security where I could slip out and vanish, he'll be raging mad.

"Well, I don't have any pain medication. Could you be a dear and get me a Panadol? I can't imagine dancing the night away if my head is throbbing like this." I offer an expression of pain, and while it's not entirely fake—my heart is deeply aching—I do have to put on a bit of an act. I rub my temples again, and Maeve smiles at me. She's the ever-dutiful doctor and I'm her sick, weak patient in need. Of course she's going to make sure she follows the letter of the law. She did recite that Hippocratic Oath.

"Of course I will." She smiles again and turns to go, and I watch her walk away, waiting until she is out of sight.

My hands work quickly, but I struggle. The way this train is attached to the dress is horrible. So many buttons and zips hide sneakily under the satin folds. I'm shaking too, racing against more than one clock. Declan could see I'm not with Loch anymore. Lochlan could wonder what's taking a while and come looking. And Maeve could return with the pain medication and I'd be screwed.

One by one, I tug at the fasteners until I decide it's not even worth it. I didn't pay thousands for this dress, but I do have multiple hundreds of thousands stashed in my father's back yard, buried in various coffee cans on the property. Besides, the O'Rourkes won't even miss this damn dress, but if I don't get out of here, I'm not even giving them a chance to miss me, and I have a point to prove.

I yank on the thick bedazzled satin fabric and hear it tear. A button skitters across the hardwood floor, and I yank again. Little by little, I work the train off the dress and lessen the weight I'm carrying. If I could, I'd race to my room and change into jeans, but if I do that, I'm risking their finding me. It will take too long.

I've only just gotten the train removed and turned toward the door when Maeve appears at the head of the hallway. She is smiling, carrying a few tablets on her palm in one hand and a glass of water in the other. Her eyebrows go up and she looks hurt as she asks, "What are you doing?"

"Sorry, Maeve, I can't do this. I know you think Ronan is so amazing, but I am not going to be trapped here against my will. I am leaving." I hike the dress up and hear the water glass crash to the ground and shatter as I start for the door. The dress is still bulky, still hard to move in, and it slows me down enough that Maeve is able to grab ahold of the bulky skirt and stop me.

I lurch forward, almost falling, and the top of the dress nearly comes down, exposing my chest.

"No, please, Isla. It's not safe. I know you want to run, but trust me. You can't do this on your own." She's pleading now? I wonder if she really does know the whole truth.

I take the hem of my dress and yank it back, trying to wrestle it away from her, but the feisty mare has a strong grip.

"Leave it," I snap, yanking hard, and she stumbles.

"Please, Isla..." Maeve isn't letting go, and my fight or flight is in top gear now.

I lunge toward her with both hands, pushing her hard until she stumbles backward into the open door of the toilet. As she begins to fall, she lets go of the dress, and I whisk it out of the door before I slam it shut. As the latch clicks, the knob falls off, which is even better. If it's broken, she can't chase me down.

"I'm so sorry," I tell her through the door, then I glance up the hallway to make sure no one hears me and I yank the dress up higher again, covering my chest more fully. And then I'm free.

Rushing up the hall toward the door, my heels click on the wood. They'll slow me down too, so I kick them off and let my bare toes feel the wood. I may not get far, and I may need to reach out to a perfect stranger for help. I know I can't go straight to my parents' house—Mum and Da are too connected to this. They won't help me until they're desperate to make sure I'm safe. So I have to lie low somewhere and sneak home to get my cash only when it's safe. Then later, when I know they'll come away, I can return to get the rest or pay someone to get it for me.

The plan plays on repeat in my head as I open the door and look around. There is no one on this side of the house, a flaw in the security plan I picked up when we did our walk-through of where all the guards would be standing last night. They made it far too easy for me to walk right out of the house, with only one hiccup. I have to get past a guard near the driveway.

The ground is cool on my toes as I run up the garden path toward the front of the house, and I hear a commotion happening around back now. No doubt,, Declan has seen that Lochlan lost sight of me. When I peek around the front corner of the house I see the guard who is supposed to be standing here is gone, chasing off toward the chaos, and I almost cry. I'm so happy.

For six weeks, I've been their prisoner. Seven, maybe—I've lost count now. And my feet carry me down the path away from this house of torture faster than I even knew I could run. They don't own me. They can't control me. I won't stay here and be someone's penance. I am my own woman. I am strong, and I'm going to fight to get my family free from the control Ronan O'Rourke exercises over them.

Finally off the property, I turn toward the sun, which I'm assuming is westward now, this late in the afternoon. I'm winded. My arms are tired of carrying the skirt of this dress, and I imagine that they're finding Maeve now in the toilet. It brings a grin to my lips to know I've bested them, and then my smile sours as I hear tires squealing.

My heart feels like it will explode. They're coming after me now. I haven't even gotten a few blocks away yet. I have no place to hide, and I can't go back. A few more strides, a few more meters away from Ronan's home, and the car comes from a direction I'm not anticipating. I'm expecting them to come from the house, to chase me down, but a long black sedan stops right in front of me and I nearly slam into it.

I move to run around it, and the door swings open, slamming into me. I hit the pavement hard and look up to see my worst nightmare. Sebastian O'Reilly's evil grin stares down at me as I suck in air and writhe on the ground in pain.

"Well, well, well... Runaway bride?" he says, then he chuckles. "Get her in the car, boys. They'll be coming."

21

DECLAN

My eyes search the crowd angrily as I stalk over to Lochlan. I see the whiskey in his hand, and before I can stop myself, I smack it away. It falls to the ground, spilling and shattering the glass, and he jerks his head up and glares at me as I press my chest into his and push him backward a few steps.

"Where is she, you eejit?" My push is a little too hard. He stumbles backward and comes back at me with both fists. Ronan stands beside me, and the shadow of his presence is the only thing that keeps Lochlan from putting a fist to my face.

"She went to the toilet. Christ almighty." Lochlan straightens his tie and takes a step back, glaring at the mess on the walk beneath my feet. They crunch in the glass as I rake a hand through my hair and glower at him.

"You let her go to the toilet alone?" I ask, seething. "Did you not see how she almost ran off during the fecking ceremony?" My brother is an imbecile, though I see it's the alcohol that's in charge right now. He probably started drinking hours ago. His words are slurred and he can't stand straight. I've been so out of my mind with trying to make sure everything went perfect that I didn't see it.

"She didn't go alone," he slurs. "Maeve went with her... They just went in there. Put the banshee on a leash if you're so worried about it." He gestures at the house as one of Ronan's men hands him a new glass.

"Just go," Ro tells me. He tightens his tie, and I turn away before I smack my other brother silly.

A few heads turn away abruptly as I stalk toward the house. They've been staring at the commotion and I'm not even ashamed of it. Almost everyone here knows how important this moment is. The security alone should be enough to discern that.

Inside the house, I fight against the flow of foot traffic, the scurry of waiters carrying trays, women ushering the last few centerpieces out, and a slew of already-drunken guests milling about. I hear Ronan drawing more attention toward Lochlan, probably for being so foolish, and ignore it. Things got substantially less dangerous the moment Isla said, "I do," but letting her go unguarded even inside this house is risky.

I know how badly she wants to flee. While I don't think any of Sebastian O'Reilly's men are brazen enough to crash this wedding, I do fear Isla will get smart and try to run off. The nervousness I saw in her eyes at that altar discouraged me. She still really doesn't want this, even after the moment we shared last night. I know she wants me. Deep down, she needs me. But she won't allow herself to believe that, and I hate it.

"Aisling, dear..." I call out, searching the hall. The closest bathroom to the door is the powder room down the side hallway. When the team carrying the cake appears at the head of the hall, I duck into the closet so they can squeeze past with mumbles of their thanks.

I force a smile and wait for them to pass, then duck back into the dim hallway and continue on. When I round the corner and see the train

THE ENFORCER'S REDEMPTION

of Isla's wedding gown lying on the floor with buttons on the wood around it, my heart freezes. A few things happen simultaneously that have my head spinning.

I hear Maeve screaming, banging on the door to the toilet. The knob's been busted off.

Then I hear gunshots and tires squealing.

A commotion out back behind me makes the hairs on my arms rise to attention. I lift a foot, shouting, "Move back!" before kicking the door open. Maeve rushes out in a puddle of mascara and tears.

"She ran... Oh, God... she ran out the door," Maeve blurts out, and I turn and run too. Her shoes are here, just inside the door that swings in the breeze.

I dart into the garden, finding women's footprints in the mud along the side of the house, and I've got my weapon drawn as I hear more gunfire coming from the front of the house. My feet can't move fast enough. My heart is pounding against my chest at the thought that she's out there now, somewhere vulnerable, somewhere scared.

As I crest the property, racing onto the sidewalk, I see Aiden and Nicholas with their guns raised, firing on a car that is racing away. From the side door of the car I see a long white swatch of material shut in the door. They've got her.

"Feck!" I scream, pointing my gun at the car, but there is traffic, and so many of our guests have their cars lining both sides of the street. The car is too far away and there's a chance my bullet could hit Isla. I can't take the shot. "Get the car!" I scream to Nicholas, but the car is parked in, covered in ribbons with tins tied to them, the words *Just Married* scrawled on the back window in white soap.

I feel a hand on my shoulder as a dozen men take to the street, and Ronan says into my ear, "We'll get her. Come on... We have to deal with guests before this gets out of hand. Mick will raise hell."

It takes every ounce of my will to turn away from that street and let our men chase them down, but Ro is right. Damage control is the first priority. Aiden and Nicholas will chase, and when things here are controlled, I'll go out too. I won't let Sebastian get away with this. His blood will be mine.

22

ISLA

My head throbs. My palms are bloody. After falling down, they dragged me into the back seat of this car. My breakfast came up, staining this gown and leaving a wretched taste in my mouth. Every time I breathe, I can smell the stench of vomit. It's never a pleasant smell, but locked in a back seat with men I know will most certainly kill me makes it seem even worse.

"You can't do this," I spit, wishing I could lash out and tear them limb from limb. They probably expect me to cower and break down crying, but I'm fighting for my life here. I don't have time to waste on tears and pleading.

"Oh but we just did, dear Princess." Sebastian is a snake of a man, beady eyes set too far apart on his head. Da told me to never trust a man whose eyes are too far apart. They're vipers, always having to watch their backs.

"Declan will—"

"O'Rourke is a spanner, born to follow someone else's commands the whole of his life." Sebastian leans forward and pushes a few strands of my hair out of my face, and I see even they're covered with vomit. It makes me shudder when his fingertips brush across my face softly. "He has no clue what he's lost."

"Fuck you," I say, drawing all the spittle in my mouth and ejecting it at him. It misses the mark I hope for and lands on his hand, not his face. But the act definitely does the trick. Sebastian recoils and then smacks me hard. My head whips to the side, and I slump into the lap of a man next to me. He grabs me by the hair and hoists me back up to a sitting position. With my hands bound behind my back, it's difficult to move, and my body aches to the bone.

Words threaten to tumble out, insults and violent threats calling upon the O'Rourke name, but I know they'd do no good. If I keep letting my mouth move when my brain knows better, I'm going to regret it. I bite back the slew of insults I'm thinking and focus my rage into a glare. Sebastian is in control right now, but I know Declan won't let that stand.

"You have something that belongs to me and I want it back," he says calmly, but the undercurrent of venom rides the words, chilling me. I will not under any circumstances lead him to my parents' home to find what I've hidden there. I will sooner die than let him connect that.

"You might as well just kill me…" I turn and stare out the window. I'm not giving them that money back now. They already have me, and there is a large chance that my death is imminent. He can get fucked.

"Oh, if only it were that easy, Princess." Sebastian folds his fingers together cooly and stares at me from his perch on the bench opposite me. The stretch limo isn't large enough for his lanky, towering body, legs so long that he finds it difficult to cross and uncross them without kicking someone. But I watch his right leg drape over his left in a comical fashion and imagine him as a skeleton with a painted skull like the men I watched dancing during Carnival in the south of Spain as a teen.

"I'm asking you to just kill me," I say tartly, but my bottom lip quivers. I don't want to die, but if it means keeping these horrible beasts of men away from my family, then I give him my permission.

"Well now," he says, resting his hands on his knee, "if you'd come to me a few hours ago, we'd have had a deal. But you see, now my hands are tied. Things just got very sticky. I'm assuming the wedding was a success?" I watch his foot roll around on his ankle and notice the expensive Italian leather they're made from. Everyone in this entire business of Mafia life flaunts their wealth. It's disgusting.

"I refused the vows," I tell him, lying. My body shudders as I squirm and try to get my hands into a more comfortable position. They're going numb. My shoulders ache. I watch out the window, but I can't tell where we're going, just that my dress is pinned in the door and even if I wanted to jump at him and attack, I can't. I'm stuck here.

"Come now," Sebastian says coolly. His eyes darken, and he glares at me with a sudden hostility that scares me. Death would be far less terrifying than this car ride. "You mean to tell me Ronan allowed you to don that dress and then not say 'I do'? He's gone weak then?"

Swallowing the bile rising in my throat again, I ignore him. If asking him to kill me quickly won't work, then pissing him off so he reacts in rage and does it might. I want him to snap and get this over with.

My mind lingers on how free I felt for a moment. I was out of that house, ready to slip into the shadows and never return, and then this. Declan's words haunt me. How many times did he warn me that I needed him and that only he could protect me? I'm a fool for thinking I could get away alone.

"Ah, so you are suddenly mute?" Sebastian uncrosses his leg and leans forward, gripping my chin and forcing me to look at him. "Tell me where my money is, you tart, or I'll bleed you dry."

"I'll never tell you." My eyes lock with his, and all I see is pure, swirling hatred weaving its way through his irises until it finds the bullseye inside my chest it's aiming for. I swallow the lump in my throat, and he squeezes harder until my jaw hurts and I wince and whimper.

"If you don't tell me—"

"What?" I snap, barely able to move my jaw to speak. "You'll do what? Kill me?" His nostrils flare as he loosens the grip on my face but doesn't let go. "The news will broadcast my nuptials to Declan O'Rourke and every family in this city will know I'm his wife. When they find out you've taken me, a war will ensue. Your alliances will go under. You'll go bankrupt. No one will work with you again, and you'll be lucky if you live a single day. Ronan will gut you like the filthy hog you are."

My threat seems to enrage him even more. His eyes flick to the man beside me, and I feel a hard blow to the back of my head, followed by the sensation of heat rushing down the back of my neck as my eyes shut.

* * *

Wincing, holding the back of my head, I blink my eyes open slowly. My body lies prone on the hard ground. It's dark in here, reeks of cigarette smoke and urine. I wish this were one of those instances where I woke not knowing where I was or what happened, wishing it were all a bad dream. But it's not.

The blow to my head in the car knocked me out but didn't erase the horror I know is true. Sebastian O'Reilly has come for what belongs to him, and I refused to give it to him. I don't know where I am, but I know it isn't a good place.

My eyes roam around the dark room and I see a streetlight outside the window. My shoulders scream at me as I push myself up off the filthy floor and attempt to stand up. I still smell like vomit, but the torn wedding gown is dry, at least. They cut my hands loose at some point, likely because they've locked me in this hellhole. I rub my wrists, and they feel raw, but not as raw as the spot in my heart that roils in regret.

A wave of nausea washes over me at the change of position and I creep to the window to peer out. I'm in some sort of house from what I can tell, but it feels like a prison. Iron bars guard the window, making it impossible for me to get out, but I manage to unlock it and slide it open enough to breathe some fresh air. That tamps the nausea down a bit, and I suck in air like it's a precious commodity.

What have I gotten myself into? And how will I manage to get myself out of this?

I shake my head and rub my eyes as I blink them into focus. The light outside leaves a ring on the sidewalk beneath it. A car rests in the glow, a mailbox, and a news stand with today's paper, probably announcing on the front page the wedding celebration of one of Dublin's most notorious criminal families. Little good it does me now.

"Someone!" I call out the window, "Help!" but I'm fearful if I scream too much, someone will come back and hit me again. Still, the chill of the air seeping in the window tempts me to try. "Someone!" I say again, but when I hear voices on the other side of the wall, I stop and hold my breath. I'm not alone here.

The voices pull me away from the window, and I touch the wall, sliding my hands along it up and down, groping for a light switch. The streetlamp outside isn't giving enough light to guide me, and I have no idea the condition of the floor here. The pads of my feet detect debris or trash. I don't want to step on anything, so I slide them along the rough carpeting instead of walking properly until I find a doorknob.

My fingers wrap around the cold metal, but I pause and listen for those voices. They don't sound angry. They sound jovial, like they're playing a game. I picture a group of men smoking cigars, seated around a table, playing a game of cards and joking with each other. My heart hammers as I grip the knob more tightly, hoping it doesn't squeak when I try to turn it. The bars on the windows keep me from fleeing that way, but surprisingly, the door isn't locked.

It clicks lightly when the knob is turned fully. The latch disengages and I pull the door back slightly, just enough to see out a crack. There is no table, no game of cards, but three men do sit in lounge chairs watching a sports show. They have open beers, and one is smoking. They're here to make sure I don't leave, and there is no way I can get past three of them.

I'm ready to shut the door and try to find a different way out when a hand appears, pressing on the door hard. It clips my chin, and I yelp as I jump back, startled. The door swings open, and I gasp in shock, covering my face and cowering against the wall, and suddenly, I'm thrust into blinding light as someone turns the ceiling lamp on. My eyes scream at the surprise but slowly adjust.

"Well, then," I hear as I uncover my face to see who's talking. Sebastian stands in front of me next to an older man who's dressed in a white Polo and khaki pants with a grey cardigan open in the front. He holds a black medical bag and wears square-rimmed glasses. "Time to make sure our princess checks out. Doctor," he says turning to the man, "you know what to do. I need to make sure she's clean."

"What?" I ask, cowering against the wall farther. But Sebastian doesn't respond to me. He turns and walks out the door, shutting it harder than necessary. I'm shivering now, trembling with fear and the chilly air now drafting into the room more quickly. "What's happening?" I ask the man, glancing at the door. I feel much safer now that Sebastian is gone, but I don't like what he said.

"You'll want to strip off, then," the man says, nodding at my gown. "I'll make sure you have something suitable to wear afterward, but I have a few exams to do." His eyes never leave my body as I shake my head in protest.

Exams? What the hell is this? And why do they keep calling me Princess?

23

DECLAN

The gates burst open with a deafening crash, a metallic groan that reverberates through the air, and we surge forward like a relentless storm unleashed. The first few shots crack through the tension, sharp and piercing, but we're already in motion, a coordinated force with no room for hesitation. We dive to the ground while the relentless roar of gunfire echoes off the compound walls like rolling thunder, a cacophony of chaos that electrifies the atmosphere.

I don't even see the first guy coming at me—just feel the hot breath of him as he charges, eyes wide with panic. Too bad for him, I'm quicker. My fist meets his jaw, snapping his head back with a sickening crack. He stumbles, and I don't waste a second. My knee drives into his ribs, then my foot slams into his gut, pushing him backward as his breath hitches.

"Keep pushing! Move in now!" Ronan roars, his voice cutting through the chaos, sending my blood racing faster. The man who tried to take me out is already crumpling at my feet. I kick him in the head once, just for good measure.

The compound's a fucking labyrinth. It's like we're walking into a maze of stone and concrete. Gunshots ping off the walls, and every movement is sharp, brutal. You can hear the men running ahead, shouts and screams mixing with the heavy crack of rifle fire.

There's no time to stop. We push forward, guns raised, the adrenaline pulsing through my veins like a fucking drug. I don't even care that I can barely see through the smoke and dust. All I care about is getting to the heart of this place, tearing it apart if I have to.

I hear Ronan's voice cutting through the madness again. "Declan! Take the left side! Don't let them regroup!"

I nod, already shifting my weight and moving. A dozen men come at me from the shadows, and I don't stop. My first shot is clean, a man down before he even realizes I'm there. The next one comes from the right. His gun cracks in the air, but I've already slid to the side, dodging it like I've done a thousand times before.

I'm on him in an instant, my fist crashing into his face with a sickening thud. His nose shatters beneath my knuckles, blood pouring like a fucking waterfall. He's done before he hits the ground. I don't even have time to breathe before another one's in front of me, swinging his fist, trying to knock me down.

Not a chance.

I duck, dodge, and the next thing I know, he's flying backward, courtesy of my elbow to his throat. He's choking, gasping for air, but I don't slow down. I'm not here to play. I'm here to fucking end this.

The sound of heavy boots slamming into the floor is all I hear before another asshole comes charging at me. This one's bigger, a mountain of a man, but that's the mistake. He's slow. He's predictable.

I catch his wrist, twisting it around before driving my knee into his gut. He stumbles, and that's when I end him—one shot to the temple. Blood splatters across the floor, his body crumpling like a rag doll.

I'm already moving before the body hits the ground, eyes scanning the chaos ahead of me. This place is full of enemies—no one's backing down, not a fucking soul. The compound's too big to clear quickly. We're surrounded. I push forward, not slowing my pace. But we're getting closer. I want to rip this place apart. I want to take it all down.

I can barely hear myself think over the blood-pumping roar in my ears. A man jumps out from behind a pillar, a knife in hand, and I'm ready. I don't need a gun for this. I grab his wrist before he can strike, twisting it until I hear the bone snap, his scream filling my ears. I slam my palm into his face, sending him crashing into the ground, and that's when I hear Ronan's voice again, sharper, more frantic.

"Declan, we need to move!"

I don't wait for him. I press forward, pushing past men, past bodies, past the fucking wreckage of whatever the hell this place used to be. There's no mercy in me anymore. There's no room for hesitation.

Then, as if the world decides to kick me in the teeth, more men appear. Five, no, six of them, their guns raised.

I don't give them the chance. My gun's already in my hand, and the first guy doesn't even see it coming. He drops like a sack of shit. The second is quicker than him, but I'm faster. I don't give him the pleasure of taking a shot. I'm on him before he can pull the trigger, my fist driving into his throat. He gasps, but I don't let him breathe.

The others try to surround me, but Ronan and Lochlan are already on it. They cut through them like a fucking machine. One by one, their bodies crumple.

We round the corner, and there he is—Sebastian, standing like he's fucking untouchable. But he's not alone. Two of his men are flanking him, guns drawn, their eyes wild. The second they see us, they take a step forward, blocking the way.

"Move," I snarl, my gun raised, but they don't budge. The air thickens with the tension of what's about to happen. There's no doubt in my mind—this ends, one way or another.

Sebastian doesn't even flinch. He stands there, looking down at us with that smug smile plastered on his face, like he's got the upper hand.

"You're not taking her, O'Rourke," Sebastian says, his voice cold, calculated.

Ronan steps forward, eyes narrowing. "We're not here to kill you. Give her up, and you walk away. We walk away. No more blood."

But Sebastian's not stupid. He's not going down without a fight. His men shift, and the tension gets even thicker. One of them twitches, but Ro doesn't give the signal to move. I know he wants as little bloodshed as possible. We're here to get my wife back, not slaughter the O'Reillys. They'll have enough hell to pay in this city from our allies when word gets out what they've done.

"Where is she, Sebastian?" I call out, and he chuckles at me. I'm seething mad and my chest is heaving from exertion, but I hold my gun steady, pointed at him. I know if I pull the trigger, there will be two shots that follow and both will be in my chest. I'm not stupid, but I'm not backing down either.

"She's not here, eejit. You think I'm stupid enough to bring that precious cargo back to my own home?" His evil laughter enrages me, and my finger twitches over the trigger. "Go home. You're only getting in the way of justice."

Justice? That bastard has the nerve to talk about justice? I'm so damn close to putting him down right there, but Ronan's hand on my shoulder stops me.

"Declan, we'll find her," he growls in my ear, his own hatred barely contained. "We'll find her, and we'll bring her home. But not like this. Not with a bullet in your back."

Damn it all to hell. He's right. I know he's right. But it doesn't stop the fury that courses through my veins, demanding retribution for every second she's been away from me.

"You think you're just going to walk away?" I spit out at him, but Sebastian only smirks.

"Today, O'Rourke. Today you do. You turn yourself around and walk right out of my home before your brother is right and I put a bullet in your back." He's a smug gobshite. I'll give him that.

"Come on, Declan. Let's go." Ronan gives the order, and I have to follow him. I hear Lochlan and the others start to retreat, but I can't help myself. I'm too angry. I drop to my knee as I pull the trigger, and it misses him, but his men don't miss. Their guns fire, and the rounds strike my shoulder and my ribcage, ripping through me with searing heat. The place erupts in gunshots again as I fall to the floor and my vision starts to blur from the pain.

I'm vaguely aware of Ronan and Lochlan dragging me back, bullets whizzing past us as we retreat. The last thing I hear is Sebastian's laughter echoing through the halls of his compound as he escapes, and with him, any hope I have of finding my wife alive.

The car ride is a blur. My chest is on fire, lava pouring through my veins as Lochlan presses on one wound and Aiden on the other. Nicholas races me to Ronan's house as I hear my brother on the phone with someone, probably Maeve, giving instructions about my injuries and what we need when we arrive.

He spits out, "Damn thick eejit, why did you shoot?" I don't see him, but I picture his head shaking at me as he glowers at me. His tone tells me the injuries aren't life threatening, but the pain slicing through my flesh doesn't seem that way.

I fade in and out of consciousness, flashes of dreams or memories haunting me. Isla was so beautiful in that dress, so perfect. I should have told her how I really feel, that I deeply love her, but I didn't, and now I may never see her again.

Mick and Brennan—they'll hate me. The alliance will suffer because of this, and all because I let her out of my sight for a mere second. This should never have happened. We should be consummating our hours-old marriage.

When I finally come to, Maeve is standing over me with a surgical mask on, blue gloves on her hands, worry creasing her forehead. She nods at someone, and my eyes shift to see Ronan standing on my other side. The blood on her gloves and his shirt is mine. I know that, and shame floods me as I realize I put my whole family at risk tonight by taking that shot.

"No one else was injured. You should be proud of yourself." He's angry, and rightly so. "What the hell were you thinking?"

"Isla," I grunt, attempting to sit up, but Maeve's bloody hand presses me down.

"Stay there. You lost a lot of blood." She twists my wrist and shows me the IV leading into my veins through the back of my hand. "You need this last unit, and you should thank Lochlan for donating." Even Maeve sounds annoyed at me, but I put Ronan at risk and I'm sure she's heard the whole story. "Stay there until I say you can get up. And then both of you need rest. You'll never find her if you're dead. You know that, right?"

"And mistakes happen when you're too tired," Ronan adds. "I'll see you at first light, and we'll go about this a different way. I already have my sources working…"

Ronan walks out, and I let my eyes flutter shut. I'm exhausted and in pain, but I'm in good hands. I just don't know how they expect me to sleep when I know what Sebastian is capable of and Isla is out there, probably terrified.

"I'm coming," I whisper to her, but I don't know if it's audible or in my dream.

24

ISLA

The dress is soaked with sweat, the fabric sticking to my skin like a second skin I can't peel away. That crude man did not give me clean clothes like he said, so I put it back on. My body aches, bruises from where they shoved me around. I'm tired, but sleep won't come—not with the way they've been treating me. I try not to think about it, but it creeps in anyway. I want to scream, but I can't. I don't have the energy.

The door slams open and one of the guards steps in, smirking. I'm shoved roughly to the side as he drops a plate of cold, congealed slop in front of me. "Eat, Princess," he sneers, his eyes glinting with some sick amusement.

I don't touch the food. I don't want to, don't even know what it is. But he's waiting, watching me with a look like he's expecting me to eat it, to beg for more. It's disgusting. I don't say anything. They call me 'Princess' like it's some kind of twisted pet name, and I don't know how to make sense of it. I'm not some pampered girl in a castle. I'm not some fucking princess.

The guard grabs my arm and jerks me back up to my feet when I don't make a move. "You think this is a fucking hotel? Eat the food. You're lucky we're feeding you at all."

His slap stings, and I stumble back, my cheek burning. Tears prick at the edges of my vision, but I blink them away. I don't give them the satisfaction.

"I'm not hungry," I say, my voice trembling despite myself.

He just laughs, a sound so cold it feels like ice. "You don't have a choice. Eat, or you'll find out how much worse it can get."

I want to scream. I want to fight back, but I know it's pointless. They won't care. I'm nothing to them, just a piece of cargo they're holding until they get what they want.

With a heavy sigh, I finally reach for the plate just to make them stop. I take a bite of the bread, and it tastes as awful as it looks.

"Good girl," the guard mocks, his voice dripping with satisfaction. "That wasn't so hard, was it, Princess?"

I want to tell him to fuck off, but I can't. The last thing I need right now is to give him a reason to hurt me more. Instead, I shove the plate away, the disgust rising in my throat.

"Don't call me that," I snap, my voice hoarse. "I'm not your fucking princess."

The guard's eyes darken, and for a second, I think he's going to hit me again. But he doesn't. He just stands there, staring at me with a sick grin. "You are whatever the fuck I say you are. Don't forget it."

He turns on his heel and slams the door behind him, leaving me alone again.

I sit there for a moment, staring at the shitty food, feeling more trapped than ever. And all I can think is, *This isn't going to end well.*

The door opens, and two women step in. One's young, probably around my age, but her eyes are old, tired. The other looks older, maybe mid-thirties, but she's just as hollow. Both of them look at me, then at the wedding dress I'm still trapped in.

"Jaysus," the younger one mutters, shaking her head. "Let's get you out of that thing."

I don't protest. I'm too numb to care about anything right now. They're gentle with me, like they expect me to break at any moment. They pull at the gown, untying it from around my body. I almost feel like I should apologize for being in the way, for being so weak, but I don't say anything. I just let them.

The older woman helps me into a faded blouse and skirt. Neither of them speaks, just moving with practiced hands. The clothes are nothing—nothing compared to what I should have. But for now, it's something. It's better than that disgusting dress.

"You should eat something," the younger one suggests, but her voice is small, uncertain. She's just trying to help. I know that. But I don't have an appetite. Not anymore.

I shake my head, the words thick in my throat. "Why are they calling me Princess?" I'm in a daze, haunted by the many, many warnings I was given to just stay with Declan. I wish now that I'd have listened to him.

The women exchange a glance. It's hard to tell whether it's sympathy or just exhaustion. They know what's coming. They've been here far longer than I have.

The older one speaks, her voice low, barely above a whisper. "It's what they do. Call you names, get you used to it." Her shoulder bobs, but the fear in her eyes betrays her. "Get you thinking you're special, just for a little while, before they take everything."

I sit there, frozen. I want to say something, but I can't find the words.

She must see it on my face because she steps closer, lowering her voice even more.

"They're getting you ready," she says, her face tight. "The doctor... the tests... They made sure you're clean." She flinches as she says it.

Clean? I want to scream, to fight, but all I can do is sit there, staring at the floor.

"Clean for what?" My voice cracks, but I already know why. My mind hasn't let me stop fearing the reason since that man touched me. The younger woman looks down, her face pale. She presses her lips together like she's weighing something—whether or not to tell me the truth, whether I can handle it.

"They're shipping you off soon," she finally says. "To Europe. To a... a sex ring. They'll sell you."

A chill crawls down my spine, a spider ready to spread its venom into my body. The blood drains from my face. I feel like I'm choking, but I can't breathe.

"No," I gasp. "No... no, that can't be..."

She doesn't look at me. The older woman steps forward, pressing her hands into my shoulders, steadying me.

"It's true," she whispers. "They've done it before. Once they take you, there's no getting out. They'll keep you locked up... like an animal."

The words hit harder than any slap they've given me. I want to break down, but I don't. I can't.

The younger woman looks at me, her eyes filled with pity, but it's all she can offer. "There's nothing we can do. Please, don't make it harder. Don't fight them." I can see the genuine concern in her eyes, but it's too little, too late.

I feel like I've lost the ability to think straight. I've heard enough. I can't breathe. I can't think. The room feels like it's closing in on me, everything spinning too fast for me to keep up. My chest tightens, my heart hammering in my ears. I try to take a step back, but the walls feel too close, too small.

I can't stay here. I can't.

Without thinking, I rush toward the door, the need to escape drowning out every other thought. The door's just within reach. I grab the handle, cold against my sweaty palm, twisting it, but before I can even pull it open, the door is shoved back in my face.

I stumble back, heart in my throat, as the men step in. They look at me like I'm a broken toy they're about to put to use.

"Thought you could run?" the first one sneers, his smirk only growing wider when he sees the panic on my face. "Where are you going, Princess?"

My chest tightens, and I can't get the air I need. They're blocking me. Both of them, massive, like they've been bred for this. They're not letting me out.

I want to scream. I want to fight, but my limbs feel like lead. My hands shake as I try to steady myself. The air feels suffocating.

When Sebastian steps into the room, the women scurry out. He nudges past his guards who stand over me menacingly and glower at me like rabid wolves being held at bay only by the Alpha who won't allow them to attack. And Sebastian knows better. At least I hope.

"Well, well… Miss Isla has a secret, no?" He chuckles a dark, sinister laugh that makes me break out in goosebumps. I hate it. I hate him.

"Go away," I tell him, fearing what the woman said is true, that he'll sell me into a sex ring and I'll never see my family again. Never seen Declan again.

"Oh, but you're much too precious now, Princess." He reaches up and touches my hair, and I feel like I may throw up on him. "The

O'Connor heir? And what will Ronan think that his brother's child will be older than his own? We'll end up with another O'Rourke scandal, won't we?"

I narrow my eyes in confusion and shake my head. I have no clue what he's talking about. I don't have a secret. There is no heir. And why would the O'Connors need an heir? My father is a normal man...

"Please, leave me alone." My voice cracks as I speak, but he doesn't back off.

"Come now, you don't expect me to believe that look of ignorance. You mean to tell me you don't know you're pregnant?" He narrows his eyes at me, and my blood runs cold.

"Pregnant?" I touch my fingers to my lips and shudder. "No..." I shake my head and back away but find my back against the wall. My head swims, and I feel dizzy, like I may pass out.

"Yes, dear... Those routine tests tell me you're clean as a whistle, ready to spread that tight pussy for any one of my dear customers." He clicks his tongue. "We'll fetch a pretty penny for you when that belly is swollen. You'd be surprised how many men love to fuck a pregnant mare." The evil grin on his face does it.

My stomach lurches, and I throw up the bit of slop I just sucked down. Then I slide down the wall and curl around my knees as he continues to speak to me.

"I imagine Declan will be very angry to find out he's lost his wife and his child in one fell swoop..." He stares down at me and then kicks my ankle. I wince and tuck my legs in tighter, wanting to cry but having nothing left in me to produce tears. "You should sleep. I hear those shipping containers are awful... And such a shame beauty like yours will be lost on some fat bloke who pays me to bend you over. You could've just given my money back."

They march out and slam the door, and this time, I hear it click. There will be no more chances for me to escape, no more visits from kind women who can answer my questions. I'm as good as gone already, and that finally brings tears to my eyes as regret stabs into my heart like a knife.

25

DECLAN

I sit on the edge of the bed where only a few nights ago Isla and I lay together. Her scent is faded from the pillow, but I held it against my chest all night anyway. This morning, Maeve redresses my wounds, changing out soiled gauze pads for clean ones. I wince when she applies pressure, but the pain now, three days later, isn't nearly what it was the night Sebastian's men shot me.

"It's looking better," she says, smearing antibiotic ointment onto the sutures she put in my flesh. The Celtic knot tattooed there is now disrupted, a scar to remind me of my almost failure, no doubt. It's poetic, almost, the symbol of our family torn through the middle by a gunshot delivered to me as I fight for my redemption. Like the final nail in the coffin of my mistake. It's behind me, and the only thing in front of me now is a war.

"I'm feeling stronger. I need to get back to the search," I tell her as I reach for my clean button-down shirt. I was able to shower this morning for the first time. Losing that much blood weakened me substantially, but I can't lie around anymore and do nothing. Ronan and my brothers have all been hard at work, using our underground team to track Sebastian's movements.

Every family in this city is now aware of what he's done. They won't take it easy on him by any means. If they hear anything, they'll rat him out immediately, but I know as well as anyone else that when this is all said and done, things will eventually fade back to normal, unlike some other feuds that have lingered for decades.

"I think you need another day," she says, pressing the surgical tape to my chest to hold the new gauze in place. "You could bust stitches if you use your arm too much." Her head shakes, tousling her hair. "You're not ready."

I scoff and scrub my hand across my beard. "I appreciate your concern, Doc, but my wife is out there and I am going to find her."

The door swings open and Ronan's hard-soled shoes clomp on the wood floor. Maeve looks up at him and scowls in concern. She understands the way things work around here and doesn't like it. We're all stubborn as mules, especially when things like this happen, though they seem to be happening more often now.

"He needs more time," she says softly as she rises from her crouched position near the side of the bed.

"We are out of time." Ronan's statement is final, and Maeve knows it. She nods once and collects her things before letting herself out. The scent of her perfume lingers, wrapping around my senses and stirring an ache for Isla I didn't realize I could even feel. My head hangs, but I slide my arms into the shirt, wincing as my muscles engage. The pain is searing, and maybe Maeve is right. I Could tear the stitches, but I can't just sit here.

"We have news..." Ronan ambles around to this side of the bed and stares up at the painting on the wall, a family portrait done for the O'Rourkes decades before I was even born. This family has a legacy of survival, and I know no matter what, we will survive this. I just want to make sure every O'Rourke survives it.

"Go on, then," I tell him as I stand and button the shirt. My chest screams for me to stop moving. Each twist of my wrist flexes the muscles that need time to rest and repair.

Ronan turns to face me with his jade-like eyes, so dark and serious now. A week ago, his only priority was confirming the wedding would happen. He would've gone as far as to let Sebastian have Isla if the alliance would go forward. But there's anger and irritation in his expression now, tight features, drawn lips.

"Mick's backing out if we don't find her. Says it's our responsibility to bring her back or the alliance won't move forward." His voice is so cold, uncaring. Losing the alliance with the O'Connor family is huge, but finding Isla should be the priority anyway, even if Mick backs out.

"It's not like we knew she was going to run." Our worry was Sebastian taking her. Ro never planned for her to be a runaway bride. "He'll come around. We just have to find her." Tucking the shirt in, I walk toward the closet where they stuffed my shoes. Everything is uncomfortable here, but I have no home to return to. It lies in ashes just like Isla's. Now we have more in common than ever.

"There's more," he says, and it chills me.

"More than losing your precious alliance?" I snip, and I know it's a bad move, but for once in his fucking life, I want my brother to feel something.

"She's the O'Connor princess, Declan. You know what that means. Every family in this city fought for the chance to align themselves to the O'Connors. Mick's legacy is legendary. When he passes, he has no son to award his entire organization. This alliance positions us to—"

"Stop it!" I shout, reeling around on him. "Just fecking stop it." My blood is boiling. "I understand it all and I don't care. The only thing that matters to me is bringing Isla home safely. That's what we focus on. The alliance means nothing to me without her. Do you understand? So if you don't find her—whatever. You lose your alliance. But I lose my heart."

My chest is heaving, hands clenched in fists. My throat constricts, and I study my chief for a few moments as he absorbs my verbal attack. I'll leave this family faster than they can draw their weapons to stop me. I have no reason to stay when I know they already doubt me. Isla is the last straw.

"She's in a shipping container at the docks, Declan." Ronan sucks in a breath and sighs hard, then he lowers himself to the foot of the bed and lets his head hang. "Da always said women are our weakness, that they soften us. But I think that's not true. I think the more you love a woman, the harder you fight to protect her and provide for her. And when there are children…"

I stoop to pick up my shoes, thankful he isn't lashing out at me after my outburst. Perhaps my brother really does have a heart in there somewhere. Maybe he's coming around to see that life is more than drug deals and selling weapons.

I plop onto the bed next to him to put my shoes on and ask, "How did we learn that?"

"The shipping container?" he asks, raising one eyebrow. "Aiden has a buddy at the docks that knows the O'Reillys' shipping schedule. Normally, it's arms and drugs. This time, it's a container full of women headed to the brothels in Eastern Europe."

I'm horrified to think that Isla is in that box with other women who've been stolen from their families too. Men like Sebastian need to be hung by their balls and stripped of their dignity.

"So he plans to hide her in a sex ring?" I scoff again and tie up the shoelaces as I shake my head. "He knows he can't kill her, so he ships her off to a life of torture where we can't find her." It's a game he's playing, one I know we'll lose if that ship sails with Isla on board. We'll never find her again.

"And there's more still," Ronan says, sucking in another deep, cleansing breath. His posture is slumped, elbows on his knees now. He scrubs both hands over his face and shocks me as he lets out an explosive scream-growl. Then he stands abruptly and takes a few long strides with his hand reared back, like he may punch the wall, but he stops himself.

I don't know what to think except that whatever game Sebastian is playing has upped the stakes substantially. I stand slowly and tug my sleeve cuffs down, waiting for him to go on. When his gaze meets mine, I see the fury there.

"What is it?"

"She's carrying the heir, Declan." He looks away, glaring at the window. "The word is, Isla is pregnant. Mick's heir, the entire reason for this alliance, to bind our families for eternity, is within reach and without her, without that baby…"

His words trail off, fading out like a whisp of smoke dissolving into thin air. Isla is pregnant? But that means it's my child. That she's pregnant with my baby and a potential heir to the O'Rourke throne. And what Mick must be going through knowing his oldest daughter is gone, taken like a commoner. And the whole time, Sebastian knew who Isla really is, and all he cares about is punishing her for making him look weak.

Ronan is right. This thing just got a hell of a lot more complex, and I can't even blame him for thinking about the alliance. Deep down, I know he cares about bringing her back, so whatever his motive for finding and rescuing her is, I'm going to side with him. My motive is personal—to ensure the woman I love is by my side for eternity. But if it benefits our family, so be it. At least my brothers are on board to fight.

"You know if it's true? If she's really pregnant?" Aiden's sources are rarely wrong. I don't know why I even doubt them. Or maybe I just need to hear it again to believe it.

"It's true." He nods curtly. "Now we have to assemble a team and get to the docks to stop that ship from leaving port, and we have to be careful. If they see us coming, there's no telling what they'll do or how many innocent people will die in the process."

The hairs on the back of my neck stand on end as I reach into the dresser and take out my gun. My wife and unborn child need me, and no one is going to stand in my way now. I will find her and I will bring her home, and I will prove to her once for all that right by my side is where she belongs.

And then I will kill Sebastian O'Reilly, if it's the last thing I do.

26

ISLA

The pulse of my heartbeat in my chest is steady but weak, and a little on the fast side. I lie curled in a ball watching a smattering of other women on the other side of the room huddled together talking quietly. I haven't eaten in four days. I'm starving, but I have no appetite. My entire body feels weak, like I've just finished a marathon or strongman contest. And I'm cold, shivering, and wishing for a blanket.

"She don't look too good," one of the women says. Her dirty skin and filthy clothes make her look like she just walked out of a coal mine, or maybe a garden digging in the soil. When she looks at me, her eyes seem to see through me, judging me silently.

"None of us look too good. Shut up." A younger woman comes to my defense, giving the first a shove. "You're alright, honey. Just rest. You'll need your energy when they move us."

I hate how they speak like they've been doing this long enough that they understand what is happening. It strips away my hope like dead skin after a sunburn, little by little whittling away at my will to live. I blink and hear my eyelids click against my eyes. Even when I sip water, it comes right back up. I know now that it's not nerves. It's morning sickness. I'm slowly starving myself and my baby to death, and I can't think of a reason to change that.

"Yeah, well with the way they carry on about her, you know…" The first woman sneers at me and picks at her tooth with her tongue. The fact that they call me Princess isn't my fault. I don't even understand it. Sebastian is a horrible man, playing mind games with me, telling me I'm carrying the heir to the O'Connor family. He's not wrong. My baby will definitely be my da's pride and joy, but we don't have a kingdom to rule over. I'm not a princess.

"Shh, don't speak about her like that." Another woman shushes them and shakes her head, spitting on the floor and performing the sign of the cross on her forehead, chest, and shoulders. Such a superstitious action. I close my eyes to pretend I don't hear them. Even they feel like this is some conspiracy or something. It exhausts me.

"Well, for some reason they think she's special, and that isn't a good thing for her."

I press my palm to my ear and block out the sounds as I replay every decision I've ever made in my life over and over in my head. Regret sucks me into a spiral that traps me there behind my eyelids, and every time I open them, it gets worse. More women populate the room. There is less space, and the stench of unwashed bodies rises.

When the door swings open and boots clomp on the ground, I fully expect it to be more women being dumped. I open my eyes to see Sebastian standing over me with a smug grin. He's wearing a white suit, a wide-brimmed white hat with a black ribbon on it, and a matching black shirt. His black patent leather shoes look recently shined, and I wish I could conjure up some stomach acid just to vomit on them.

He crouches next to me and pushes the hair off my face. "How is the princess fairing?" he asks, and I squirm away from his touch. The women in this room are dead silent, but I hear them rustling around, also uncomfortable with his presence. "What, you don't like me?" He feigns innocence, and I search my mouth for moisture to spit on him but my mouth is bone dry. I'm far too dehydrated.

"You are the wife of my enemy, so I can't kill you. But it doesn't mean I can't sell you to get back what you stole from me." He remains crouching next to me, chuckling like a madman. Then says, "In a few days' time, you'll have a new home with lots of new friends and plenty of work. I hope you're in shape."

"Screw off," I snip weakly. It comes out in a ragged, scratchy tone I don't recognize, but it's my own voice. It draws gasps from some of the other women in the room who clearly would never stand up to a man like him. But I have nothing to live for. I can't imagine letting this baby I'm carrying come into the world like this. Who knows what they'll do to him or her? And that cements my will to die.

"You have a temper, Princess, and it's going to get you in trouble." Sebastian stretches out his hand, and I push it away, but he's stronger than me. What appears to be another attempt to touch my hair turns into me guiding his hand toward my mouth where I bite down hard enough to draw blood.

"You cunt!" he screeches, then smacks me hard. I scramble as far away from him as I can on the filthy mattress, pressing my back to the wall. But Sebastian grabs my leg and pulls me back toward himself. Blood drips from his thumb as he wraps his thick fingers around my throat and squeezes. "You're damn lucky you walked down that aisle." His grip is so tight I'm seeing stars. I grab his wrist with both hands, trying to pry him away from my neck, but he is relentless, clamping down to the point that I can't breathe.

I gasp and choke, hearing the other women in the room also murmuring and gasping too. My eyes blink rapidly, filling with moisture that leaks out onto my cheeks and runs down onto the mattress under me. My chest screams for air as it burns and heaves to suck in a breath. I mouth the words, "Please stop," but the sadist won't let go of me. He only squeezes harder.

My eyes shut, and I pray they'll never open.

* * *

A loud noise startles me awake, a hollow crash of metal on metal. I jerk upright and regret it. My head slams into something hard and makes me wince. It's pitch black. I can't see a thing, but I sense I'm not alone. The same murmuring of voices and the stench of filthy bodies meets my senses, and I reach out and grope in the darkness.

"Hey, there, watch it." A woman's voice greets me, her tone angry.

"Where am I? What's going on?" I say, still groping in the darkness. My hand finds another person, this one kinder. Their hands clasp onto mine and calm me.

"I told ye we were being moved, dear." The same younger woman who spoke kindly about me in that room is here. But where is here?

"I don't want to move," I whimper, and then I cough. My throat hurts. It feels like my neck is collapsed in on itself, which makes me remember Sebastian's hand wrapped around me, squeezing the life out of me.

"'Fraid we don't get a choice," I hear, and something sparks, a light or a flame. I focus on it until I see the face of the woman behind the light. I've never seen her before. She's my age, at least, maybe slightly older, with dark blue eyes. She holds up a candle to the flame, which I can see is from a match, and the candle ignites. "They ship us all over the world in metal boxes like this. You get used to it. I learned to be prepared," she says, nodding at her candle.

In the dim light I can see several other faces, though the glow doesn't show me the entire space. I hear more people talking too, farther away. This has to be a shipping container like they put on boats and trains to transport cargo. Those women weren't kidding. Sebastian is really selling us like we're livestock.

My body shudders as I spin around and see a woman behind me nursing her head. That's probably what I ran into when I jumped up so quickly. I feel bad for that, but how was I supposed to know we'd be stacked up in here like sardines, or that we'd be in here at all?

"No, they can't just sell us. We're not property." My legs are weak, but I push myself upward and lean on the cold metal wall for support. "We have to find a way out."

A few of them chuckle. Others whose faces I can see in the candlelight look scared. I can tell for some of these women, it's not their first time doing this. It sickens me.

"Ain't no way out, Princess," one of the women spits, and I sense her hostility. I recognize her voice too, from the room.

"I'm not a fecking princess." Slamming my hand on the wall, I scream as loud as I can, "Help! Someone help us!" The blows hurt my arms and wrists, but I smash my hands over and over against the thick metal, making my already hoarse voice worse.

"Yer wastin' yer time. Ain't no one gonna hear ye." The angry woman stands and grabs my arm, shoving me back into my place. I fall to my ass and curl into a ball, and a strange sensation washes over me.

I don't want to die. I don't want to give in to the consuming fear that I'll never see my family again, that my child will be born into this slave trade where women are abused and molested. I can't let my hope die. I have to believe Declan and Ronan will come and find us, that they'll stop Sebastian and his men from selling us like whores.

Some of these women look young, too young. I know the O'Rourke men would never do something like this. I know if I had just stayed with Declan, I'd be safe too. Our child, which I would've eventually discovered, would have a loving home, a safe home.

"Ain't no one out there to hear ye neither." She sits back down, and the whoosh of air as she does makes the candle's flame dance.

"You're wrong. Declan is coming. He'll stop Sebastian from doing this and he'll save us." I tuck my chin to my knees and clamp my eyes shut. If I had any water in my body, it would turn to rivers on my cheeks right now.

"Yer man ain't gonna save ye. If he was, why'd he let ye go, anyway?"

The woman's cynicism detonates something inside my chest and I feel my hope come to life. "You're wrong. I know you're wrong. You'll see. Declan O'Rourke will die before he allows me to be sold off like a slave. He'll be here. And you'll eat your words." My eyes lock on the face of a girl who can't be much older than Rebecca, and I see that my words are giving her hope too.

She doesn't break eye contact with me at all until the flame of the candle snuffs out and we're plunged into darkness again. But even the blackest night can't extinguish the truth rising up in me. A war will break out, and Declan will fight to the death to find me. It's the only thing I can let myself think. He will come.

He has to.

27

DECLAN

With the car rumbling down the highway toward the docks, it's hard to think straight. I have so much adrenaline coursing through my body right now, I don't even know what calm is anymore. Sebastian stole my wife, and all I can think about is getting her back and destroying him.

"How will we find the right container?" Lochlan asks. He's seated next to me in the back of the car. Nicholas is driving, Brynn in the passenger seat. Lochlan chambers a round in his gun and drops his clip to replace the one round from the clip to ensure his gun is fully loaded.

I've already done that on all three of my weapons. And I have an extra clip for each one. After that showdown at Sebastian's compound, I'm not taking any chances. I rub my sore shoulder absently as I answer him.

"Aiden's man at the docks narrowed it down for us. It'll be on dock seven for sure. That's where O'Reilly always ports his ship." I rub the back of my neck, my palms sweaty. My foot bounces, bobbing my knee rapidly. We're not alone. Ronan and Connor each have a car full of men, and Finn will join us at the docks with Aiden and another group. If Sebastian suspects our coming, this could be a full bloodbath.

"So what, we just shoot them up or...?" Brynn is an idiot. His question angers me.

"Shoot them up? There are people in those containers. My wife is in one. Why the feck would I shoot them up?" I need to rein in my temper or I'm going to lose it on him before we even get there. He's lucky he's even allowed to come along with me. I should've split his skull after that stunt he pulled going behind my back to Ronan.

"We'll listen..." Lochlan's voice is low and even. He has no emotions at stake in this. His purpose is to keep me in check and make sure our alliance is restored. I appreciate that he's here because I'm ready to take no prisoners, and I need his more even keel to do this correctly. "Once we get through security, there will be a ruckus, I'm sure. Sebastian's men won't like us just showing up. We'll end up making noise, and when the women in that container hear it, they'll scream for help."

His gaze is concentrated on the road ahead. He acts like this is something we do every day, like he's seen it so many times it's old hat. It's the first time we've ever attempted something this brazen, to storm an enemy's territory and openly steal from them under cover of darkness. And tonight is especially dark.

"And if we don't hear them?" Brynn's eyes meet mine in the mirror on the back side of his visor. I can see his wheels turning, still scheming. He won't stop until he pushes me too far now because he knows Ronan is confident in me. He'll never have my position, and he hates that.

"We'll hear them," I grunt, and the car slows as Nicholas pulls up to the security gates surrounding the dock access point.

The guard walks out of the guard shack. He's a hulk of a man, towering to at least six and a half feet tall. His chest is covered by a

Kevlar vest, a gun on his hip and another on his chest. He probably has mace and a few knives tucked away too, and a radio is strapped to his chest on the left side. He strolls right up to the car as Nicholas lowers his window and leans down to peer inside the car.

"Evening, gentlemen," he says calmly, but I sense an edge of hostility in his tone. Aiden's man said we may have trouble getting through the gate, but this dumb fucker doesn't know I'm willing to do anything to get Isla back. Including putting a lead slug into his brain if he tries to stop us.

"Evening, sir," Nicholas responds. "We just have some business at dock seven." His voice is tight and stiff. He's no stranger to this type of situation. I imagine his hand rests on the butt of his gun holstered at his hip just like mine.

"I'll need to see some sort of ID, please." The guard's eyes flick to meet mine then narrow at me. "What sort of business?" I watch his fingers twitch, his nostrils flare. The bastard is going to call for more security or something. I can see it in his eyes. He has to be on Sebastian's payroll.

Before he can even flinch, my gun is out and aimed at his head. He grips the side of the car as both Lochlan and Nicholas also raise their guns.

"We are going in, with or without your permission," I tell him, but then I get a better idea. This man might be able to help us narrow down the search even more. If he works for the O'Reillys, he might know which container has the women.

I nudge Lochlan, and he opens the door. With three guns—and Brynn's very slowly raised fourth—on him, the man can only straighten and keep his hands raised in surrender. We both slide out of the car on his side, and I walk over to him and put the gun against the side of his neck.

"Hand my driver your weapons," I tell him calmly, and the man complies with me. He doesn't twitch or whimper. His hands are steady, and his breathing is still calm and shallow as he slips the weapons out of their holsters and into Nicholas's hands. "Now tell me what you know about Sebastian O'Reilly," I order, but suddenly, the man is tight-lipped. He presses his lips into line and his nostrils flare again.

"If you know what's good for ya, you'll tell him." Lochlan leans against the side of the car and glances back at the row of black sedans behind us. Ronan is there, Connor, and it appears Aiden's car has just brought up the rear. My entire family has turned up to help me end this thing once and for all.

"He runs out of dock seven. That's all I know." The man's dark skin is beading with sweat. It's not even a hot night. He's just terrified. He knows I'll kill him.

"Does he ship women?" I ask, pressing the tip of my gun against his neck harder. Brynn climbs out of the car and rounds the front of it to join me with a menacing expression on his face. I can handle this, but he's got to show me up. "Answer me!" I snap when the man is slow to respond.

"How the feck am I supposed to know what the bastard ships? He just pays me to keep an eye on the gate and tell him who comes and goes. This is a public dock, you know?"

My temper flares, and I use the butt of the gun to smack him hard on the back of the head. He crumples to the ground in a grunt, holding the spot I smacked, and I pull off my tie and start lashing it around his hands. Dragging him to the gate shack, I use his badge to open the door. Brynn follows along behind me, kicking the guard every few strides.

"Knock it off," I bite out, but Brynn continues anyway.

Inside the gate shack, I lash the man to the leg of the counter that's bolted to the ground. Then I look around his body for some sort of key or badge that might let me open this gate. We could ram it, but we need the car in working order to get out of here.

"Look for a key or something," I snap at Brynn as Lochlan walks through the door. I glance up to see him standing over the guard.

"You guys are gonna get me fired. You can't do this." The guard earns another kick from Brynn, which I ignore. I pull his wallet out, sort through it, toss it to the side, and then put my gun back to his chin.

"How do we open the gate?" I demand, and he shakes his head.

"Uh-uh, no way." He grits his teeth as I shove the gun harder against his jaw from below.

"Open the fucking gate," I say in a growl, and his eyes nervously flick toward Lochlan. Behind my brother on the wall is a large red switch. It makes me crack a smug grin. "Thank you," I tell him, and I give him another hard knock to the head before standing up.

Loch moves out of the way as I reach for the switch. When I flick it, the gates outside start to roll open, the large chain link contraption retracting on itself. Lochlan nods at me and darts through the door toward the car, and I gesture for Brynn.

"Let's get out of here," I snap, just as Brynn's gun discharges.

The guard's blood sprays all over the floor and metal desk. It splatters the window and begins to pool around the guard's body.

"What the feck?" I growl, aiming my weapon at him. "Why'd you do that? You didn't need to kill him. We got what we wanted."

"Loose lips sink ships, Declan. Do your fucking job." Brynn starts to walk past me as I stare down at the dead guard, the mess of his wallet on the ground next to him. There's a picture of him holding a child, standing next to a beautiful woman. He had a family.

My gun feels heavy in my hand as I raise it up and point it at Brynn. He stops and looks me in the eye as I aim it right at his forehead. "The men in this family do not just murder anyone who looks at them wrong." My hand holds steady, fingers itching to put this bastard in the ground. Instead, I walk forward until my gun's nose is pressed right to Brynn's forehead. He leans into it.

"Are you gonna kill me, then?" he asks me, and I clench my jaw, willing myself not to do this right in front of my brother and half the family lined up in those cars.

"Fuck up again and I'll do worse than kill you. I'll make you wish you were dead." I slide my gun to the side of his head and pull the trigger. The boom makes him wince, and he shouts loudly, covering his ear. Even if the blast didn't deafen him, he'll definitely think twice about crossing me again.

Stomping back out to the car, I climb in next to Lochlan. Nicholas waits for Brynn to climb back in and then takes off. All four cars parade across the property until we see the docks marked clearly as dock seven. One by one, the cars empty, my brothers flanking me and Ronan as we lead the charge.

"You sure this is the right place?" Connor asks me, and I nod.

"I'm sure," I say, and I am. Someone's going to pay for taking my family, and I'm prepared to make them hurt.

Our group moves quickly and stealthily toward the large, stacked containers, guns raised and ready for anything. It's silent all around us except for the water lapping against the docks and the creaking of the ships moored at their berths. As we creep closer, I can just make out voices inside one of the containers. I doubt it's the women, and as I peer around the corner, I see a few men smoking cigarettes and talking.

"In there," I whisper, pointing to a container that has a line of men in front of it. Lochlan, Connor, and Ronan flank me as we approach.

Nicholas and Aiden take the other side with Brynn reluctantly following.

"On my signal," I mouth, and they all nod in agreement. "One, two, three!"

We round the corner at once, catching the men by surprise. The element of surprise is on our side as we open fire without mercy. Men fall left and right, their cries muffled by the sound of gunfire. A few of them get a couple of rounds off, but they're mercilessly slaughtered anyway. I step over a body to reach for the door, but it's locked, not budging.

"Over there!" a man shouts, and instantly, there is a hail of bullets pinging against the containers all around us.

We all take cover, crouching around the corners, ducking behind barrels. Finn hides behind the tow motor and lets a few rounds rip out of his gun, and I take aim on more of Sebastian's men as they race toward us.

"We're pinned down!" Connor shouts, and I swear under my breath.

"Lochlan, take the left side, Finn the right. We'll provide cover!" I yell over the gunfire. Lochlan and Finn nod and bolt out from their hiding spots, spraying bullets as they go.

A bullet whizzes past my head, and I duck low behind a crate. There's a scream, and I peek my head up to see Brynn staggering backward, his chest covered in blood.

"Dammit!" I scream, scrambling to my feet. We can't afford loss of life, and the crimson stain blossoming on his shirt tells me it's bad. "Fecking stay down," I tell him, shoving one of my spare weapons into his hands for self-defense. I drag him behind the crate and continue on my mission to knock down as many of these men as I can.

Lochlan and Finn have thinned out the herd, but more keep coming. I duck behind the corner of the container, breathing hard as I reload my weapon.

A hand grabs my ankle, and I whip around, ready to end whoever it is. It's one of Sebastian's men, clutching at his stomach. I point my gun at his face, prepared to send him to hell when he speaks up.

"I know where they are!" he gasps, blood bubbling from his lips.

"Where?" I demand. He points to a container farther down the docks, and I nod.

"Finn! Lochlan! We got a lead!" I yell over my shoulder as more gunfire erupts behind me.

I hope that poor bastard knows what he's done. I have mercy on him and let him live a few more minutes at least as I dart down the pier toward the dark blue container, praying Isla is there. That I'm not too late.

28

ISLA

My eyes have grown accustomed to the darkness now. There is no way of telling whether it's day or night. Not a sliver of light seeps through the thick metal walls of this container. Esther, the woman with the candle, lights this place up every so often, which is a small relief, but the darkness doesn't scare me as much as it initially did.

My nose has become blind to the scents too. I know we must stink to high heaven. There is no place to pee and every so often, the rank stench of urine meets my nose, but even that quickly fades into the atmosphere of what must be the grossest smell on the planet.

When someone passes me a piece of crusty bread and some warm cheese, I pass. The texture in my fingers is enough to tell me I don't want to eat it, but passing on it doesn't stop my stomach from churning. Bile forces its way up into my throat, and I vomit on myself. Luckily, I haven't eaten in days so there's only a small mess.

I'm leaning on the wall, pressing my face to the cold metal as I close my eyes. The only thing about me that isn't weak is my sense of hope that Declan and Ronan will come get us out of here. I know that for whatever reason, my marrying into the O'Rourke family was desperately important, and now after hearing bits and pieces of things I'm not sure I understand, I wonder if there's more to it than just my taking his name.

"Get off me," someone grumbles, and I hear someone else yelp. There's a bit of a scuffle at the far end of the container before it calms again.

Sleep starts to come, playing at the edges of my consciousness for a few languid seconds as I think morbid thoughts of death and suicide. If they don't come, I'll chew through my own arm or something, anything to stop the inevitable from happening. I won't be traded like a whore, and I will never allow my baby to be born into this world and stolen from me, sold off to the highest bidder. Or worse, they could kill my baby.

Just as I feel myself starting to doze, I think I hear the rapid pop of gunshots. My mind is foggy with sleep, hazy with a dream tempting me into its embrace. Declan, shooting his way through a crowd of men to rescue me, throwing his arms around me and kissing me passionately, my father there, cheering him on. But a voice startles me, and I jerk awake.

"What's that sound?" one of the women asks. She's sitting far away from me, but her voice reverberates down the narrow space to reach me.

"Yeah, it sounds like fireworks..." Another voice from the darkness.

"Oh, God," I mumble, covering my mouth. I sit straighter and listen, but their murmurs cover the sound. "Shh!" I hiss at them, and the container goes silent. Pressing my ear to the wall, I listen again, and there's no mistaking it. The rapid pop, pop, pop echoes again, and I shoot to my feet, slamming my palms on the wall and screaming, "Help!"

"Sit down. Shut up! No one's coming for you," someone says. I think it's that nasty bitty from the room back at that house, and I don't pay any attention to her.

"They're here! I knew they'd come. It's Declan. He's coming." My chest vibrates with energy. I continue smacking the wall, shouting at the top of my lungs. Soon, other women join me in the ruckus, chanting and pounding on the container. The noise is so loud, I can't tell if the gunshots have stopped, but the only way to let them know where we are is to make noise.

"Don't stop! Keep shouting," I coach them before sucking in a breath. I'm so winded and weak. My arm wants to give out, to droop to my side and rest. But if he hasn't stopped fighting for me, I can't give up either.

He should have. As much as I've fought him and resisted everything he offered me, Declan should have given up and let me die, let them take me. I know my father would never have stood for it. He'd have gone to the police to get help, but it would've been too little, too late. To fight men like Sebastian O'Reilly, you need to fight fire with fire, and Declan is the only man for the job.

After a few more long minutes of pounding, I have to stop. My hands are throbbing, my chest heaving for air. I lean on the metal and suck in huge gulps of putrid air into my lungs. I can't breathe and I feel dizzy, but I manage to blurt out. "Okay!"

The clatter dies down slowly, and we're left with only the sound of shuffling bodies in the darkness. For a moment in the silence, fear creeps in, telling me they've gone and we've lost our chance to be rescued. I want to cry as I again press my ear to the wall.

But the sound of men's voices is there now, and they're close.

"Declan! Ronan!" I scream, "Help!" and instantly, I get a reply.

"Isla?"

"Declan," I whimper, letting the emotion well up in my chest. "Help, please... Get me out of here." A rush of energy pushes me back up to my full height. I feel the wall, hoping to find a latch or lock.

"Stand back from the wall, Isla," he orders, and as one, the women lurch away. I stumble, but strong arms hold me up, and whoever it is, I'm grateful for the support.

Seconds later, a gun erupts again, this time with a deafening crack and the ping of a bullet hitting metal. Two shots more, and the door pops open. Light streams in, though it's still dim, but brighter than I've seen in hours. I rush to the open door and push it as Declan pulls it open, and I fall into his arms, weeping.

The tears are hot and fast, and I can't stop them. I'm shocked I even have enough hydration in my body to make tears. His arms wrap around me firmly. He places kisses on my cheeks and forehead.

"I'm here," he comforts. "Hey, shh. It's okay now. I've got you."

I cling to him for the life preserver he is, and a new sound pricks my senses—sirens in the distance.

"We need to go," Declan says softly in my ear.

I turn to look over my shoulder at the women filing out of their cage. My heart aches for each and every one of them, even the particularly nasty ones who swore we'd never be rescued.

"What about them?" My eyes search their faces, memorizing each one of them, promising to never forget them.

"The cops will be here any second and will help them, Isla, but we have to get out before we get caught." He holsters his gun at his hip, and I nod at him. My legs falter as I start moving, so he picks me up.

It slowly registers to me as my eyes adjust to the brightness of the streetlamps that the entire family is here. Men I've never met, a few of my father's farm hands, all come to save me.

"My God," I say, clinging to his neck. I nuzzle my face into the crook and press my eyes shut. "I knew you'd come."

"O'Rourke!" I hear, and it makes my blood run cold. It's Sebastian's voice.

"Mother of God," Declan grunts as he ducks behind one of the containers. He sets me down and presses his palms to my cheeks. "Stay down. Do you hear me? Let me handle this."

The others are still running, racing across the parking area toward their cars in the distance, but Declan turns around and holds up a gun.

"Show yourself, scumbag," Declan shouts, and Sebastian fires off his weapon.

I fall to the ground and cover my ears as yet another volley of gunfire erupts. Every shot makes me jump until I lose count of how many booms explode around me. When I hear tires squealing and feel Declan jerking me off the ground, I open my eyes and see a car. Thank God, I'm saved.

My salvation comes in the same form Declan prophesied. He will protect me. I just have to trust him, and now I do.

We dash to the car, and his driver zips away into the night, but all I can do is melt into Declan and cry tears of joy as he kisses my face.

29

DECLAN

Finally back to the safety of Ronan's home, I carry Isla across the threshold, the way I should've done days ago, and up to the room he prepared for us to stay in until I find a new home suitable for protecting and growing my family. My strong arms hold her as if she's nothing. It's only been a few days, but it feels like she's lost weight. She's weak, clinging to me, crying softly in a way I've never seen her do before. Sebastian broke her, and I'm anxious to find out how badly.

"We're home now, for a while, anyway," I say to her softly. My lips press kisses to her forehead and temple as I climb the stairs. "And we'll stay here until we decide what to do next."

If it were up to me, I'd go house shopping tomorrow, perhaps buy some land outside the city on a large, sprawling farm like Mick's so that my son or daughter will have a safe haven to grow up in. But it's not up to me.

Sebastian didn't just take Isla.

She ran off.

Her wandering, frightened heart had so much pressure on it, she was never given the opportunity to adjust and accept the facts. They were forced on her. People hid the truth, her father and my brother.

Right now, she's in no shape to learn it all, and after being with Sebastian, I don't know what to think or what she knows. All I know is I have her safe in my arms and I don't ever want to let her go. It shatters my heart to think that she may still want to escape, but now as my bride, with the alliance secure again, if she wants to leave, I have to make a way for her to do it. Love demands that of me.

"Are you hungry? Have you eaten? Thirsty?" My questions are returned with sniffles and a shrug of her shoulder. I don't know how they treated her, what they might have done to her. I don't even know if she knows that she's pregnant yet, if anyone told her.

When I set her on the edge of the bed and kneel in front of her, she looks me in the eye and places her palm on my cheek. "I knew you'd come for me," she says softly, blinking out a few more tears.

My hands cup her hips. I drop my head to her lap for a moment, breathing in the feeling of relief that she's back in my protection. "I would never let them take you, Isla." My voice is muffled by the fabric of the faded skirt she wears, clearly not her own clothing but something they forced her to put on. Her fingers tangle in my hair and she scratches my scalp.

"I'm sorry for running away," she sobs, and it draws me up to pull her into my chest.

"Hey, no... I'm so sorry you were forced to go through all that. We all should've known better. You deserved better, and I'm here to give that to you now. You are my wife, Isla, not Mick's daughter, not Ronan's employee. As my wife, now I make the choices for you." I cup her cheek and brush the tears from her bruised skin. Her eyes are full of sadness and pain. It makes me want to go back to those docks and gut Sebastian O'Reilly with a spoon.

"Thank you for saving me... and...." Her head drops, and I watch her slide her hand across her belly. When she lifts her eyes, they're searching my expression.

"I know, baby..." It doesn't feel appropriate, but I smile. "I know. We're having a baby, and it makes me the happiest man alive." I say those words with hesitancy, not sure how she feels about being forever linked to my bloodline. After knowing how she's felt for two months now, she could honestly hate the entire idea.

She says nothing for a moment, but when I press my lips to hers, she returns the kiss. Then when she pulls away, she says, "Are you sure?"

I'm not certain what that is supposed to mean, so I give her the only answer I can. "I want a family. I want you as my wife, and not because of some alliance but because I love you. I've never loved anyone but you." My hand covers hers on her belly. "And I want this baby, and I don't want any of this if I don't have you." Blinking, I add, "And if you still want to run away and find freedom, I will make sure it happens."

Isla shakes her head and closes her eyes. Rivers form on her cheeks. She covers her mouth with a hand and sobs quietly, then throws her arms around me and whispers, "I love you too." The words hit my chest harder than those bullets, the wounds of which are still healing, but instead of pain, I find healing. "And I want you too."

My hand rises to the back of her head, and I crush her against my body, breathing in her scent, the vomit, urine, and body odor. It's all heavenly to me, simply because she is in my arms. For better or worse, richer or poorer, sickness and in health, until death do us part, she's mine.

After a few moments, I pull away and use the pads of my thumbs to wipe the rest of the tears off her cheeks. She must be starved and exhausted, but she is still every bit as gorgeous.

"I'll draw you a bath, and then you should eat..." I rise, and she clings to my hand.

"But Mum and Da…" The pain on her face seeps through her words, pulling my heartstrings.

"They know you're safe. You don't want them to see you this way. Let's clean up, and after you've rested, we'll go visit them. Or if you'd like, they can come here. You're the queen now." The corner of my mouth lilts in a smile, but she narrows her eyes. Still, she rises and follows me into the bathroom.

I stoop to draw her a bath, and she slides the skirt and her soiled panties off, immediately tossing them into the trash bin. While the water begins to fill the clawfoot bath, I turn to help her take off her shirt. She winces as she lifts her arms, and when the tatty fabric of the faded T-shirt is off and her skin is exposed, I see why. She's bruised all over her body.

It makes me feel instantly enraged. I will get revenge on Sebastian for this. And it makes me feel so protective of her. I touch a bruise lightly and then hold her arm gently as I ask, "They hurt you?" The horrors she's seen probably outweigh anything I have ever been through. I'm terrified they've done more than just smack her. My face must express it because she sighs and rests a palm on my chest.

"Not like that, Declan. They just manhandled me, hit me a few times." By the looks of it, it was far more than a few times, but I don't question her.

"I'll kill him," I tell her, and she lays her head on my chest.

"I love you." Her arms wrap around my middle, but I pry them away and help her climb into the tub. It's large enough for both of us, but I kneel at the side for the moment. I won't take that liberty unless she asks me, but having her back, seeing her skin purpled with trauma, it makes me fiercely possessive, gives me a craving to consummate this marriage and show everyone in this world that she's mine, and I will kill for her if I have to.

Isla sinks into the water and I shut it off. She reclines, letting her body relax under the surface. Her eyes shut as she lays her head back, and I unbutton my shirt and remove it. I can't very well help her wash or massage the tension from her body with my sleeves in the way. When she hears me toss the shirt away, she opens her eyes.

"Joining me?" she asks, and I see the hint of desire in her eyes.

"We don't have to do that tonight, Isla. I want to take care of you. You've been through so much." I reach for a wash rag under the sink and return to wet it, lather it with soap. I move to begin washing her skin, and she grabs my wrist.

"I want to do that tonight," she says meekly, "with you." Her eyes lock on mine. "And every night from now on. You're my husband. Are you telling me you'll deny me?"

The faintest smile curls her lips, and I grin like an idiot. Just at her showing any interest in me at all, my cock has gone rock hard. I leave the wash rag in the water to sink against her body, and I stand up, kicking off my boots. My pants and boxers join my soiled shirt, and Isla leans forward in the bath so I can slip in behind her. She sits between my legs for now, leaning on my chest as I retrieve the wash rag and start washing her clean.

Her skin is so tender, I'm not sure where to even touch so I don't hurt her, but she revels in my touch, guiding my hands to her tits, then between her legs. Once shaven clean, she now has stubble, and I take a razor perched on the stand next to the tub. She lets me shave her and wash her, and as I do, her moisture builds. Its thick, sticky texture is vastly different from the water we're submerged in.

"Touch me," she whispers, sliding my fingers between her folds, and I set the razor to the side and kiss the side of her neck.

Isla grinds against me softly, my cock pinned between her back and my pelvis, then she sinks under the water, soaking her hair before rising back up and forcing my fingers to begin rubbing her clit.

It's so sensual and slow, so different from the past sexual experiences with her. I like it, though I can't wait to dominate her again.

I rub her clit as she spreads her legs as wide as she can in this tiny bath.

I slip two fingers inside her, and she moans, her head falling back against my chest.

"Oh, Declan... f–faster..." she pants, and I oblige her. My thumb now rubs her clit in circles as my pointer and middle finger penetrate her, searching for that spot. The water sloshes around us as she writhes against my dick, making it harder. Her body tenses and goes rigid, and I bite her neck hard. She shudders and cries out as she comes with a muffled moan, her vaginal walls clenching around my fingers.

I pull my hand free of the water, bring it to my lips, and lick it clean before kissing her neck. The water has washed most of it away, but I can still taste her delicious flavor. "You're delicious," I tell her huskily, "and you're mine."

"Yes," she moans. "I'm yours, Declan. I've always been yours."

When she presses her hands against my thighs and begins to lift herself up, I think she's going to get out. Instead, she hovers, waiting for me, so I hold my dick upright, sliding it along her folds, and she lowers onto it with a satisfying grunt of pleasure.

"Isla," I groan, my eyes rolling back in my head, "fuck, you're so tight."

I reach around her and grab her tits as she begins to move on top of me, up and down on my dick like she's riding a horse. She moans, throwing her head back as she takes me deeper and deeper. I can feel her walls squeezing me, milking my cock as we fuck.

"Oh, fuck," I groan. "Isla... You feel so good... So fucking good."

It's loud, water sloshing around, but her body is better than ever. She grips my thighs and continues riding me, rising until my cock almost springs out of her, then sinking down until I hit her back wall. Her pussy feels so incredible, and I guide her movements with my hands on her hips.

"Yes, baby… Like that… That's it…"

Her moans are music to my ears, her pussy milking me, and I feel myself getting close.

"I'm c-close," she gasps. "Oh, fuck… I'm—"

I pull her hips down so she takes me all the way in, and she keens, her pussy tightening around my dick. I moan as I orgasm inside her, releasing my seed deep in her womb. She convulses and jerks. I grip both of her tits and pull her back against my chest and push deeper into her core. Her pussy pulses rhythmically around me, and I bite down on her shoulder again. Feeling the waves of pleasure course through her in this position is erotic, but claiming her as mine, once for all, knowing she wants it as much as I do—that's the part that satisfies me.

Isla is mine, and no one will ever take her from me again. I just hope she doesn't completely flip out when we tell her the whole truth. That Mick O'Connor's legacy is darker and more dangerous than anything the O'Rourkes have ever done, and she was the key to saving his soul from the devil.

30

ISLA

The bed is cold when I wake up. I'm alone. Declan has slipped out at some point, and my exhaustion has carried me straight through to morning. Sunlight streams in the windows. I hear birds singing, and it feels good to be alive. Except for the awful nausea tainting my stomach yet again.

This time, however, I know it's due to the little one I'm carrying and not nerves over a wedding or terror from being imprisoned by horrible men. It makes me smile to think I'm going to be a mother, and I am thankful for the morning sickness that reminds me that life is good. I'm alive, and I have a fierce man who will always make sure I'm safe.

Pushing myself up on the bed, I remember the conversation I had with Declan after I had a bit of food and some water last night. I don't know what time it is, but he promised to have my parents here first thing in the morning. I'm sure they're sick with worry, Rebecca too. I wonder if she'll come. My running off had to have given them the scare of a lifetime. I know it traumatized me, and I'll be working through some heavy emotions for weeks to come.

I slip out of bed and rush to the toilet to relieve my bladder. It's the first time I've had to pee in so long. I was so dehydrated, but Declan insisted I drink until my belly was bursting. I'm thankful he cares for me and hovered last night.

I see someone has laid out a toothbrush and toothpaste, some deodorant, a brush, and a small bottle of lotion. It makes me smile to think the large, hulking madman who guns people down, to whom I am now consummately married, is thoughtful like this. No one would ever know it judging by his appearance or reputation, but he's a romantic at heart.

After pampering my skin with the lotion and brushing my teeth, I rake the brush through my hair, slap on some deodorant, and walk my naked body back into the bedroom. When we came here the night before the wedding, the night Declan's home was burned to the ground, I brought only a few things with me. I had no intention of staying with him forever. I packed light, expecting him to force me off on some ridiculous honeymoon if my attempt to flee failed.

Now I wish I'd have had more forethought. I pluck the only thing I brought with me out of the dresser—a pair of stretch pants and a white cotton shift that falls to mid-thigh. No panties, no bra, but I'm covered, and if I know my husband, he'll send for a wardrobe fit for a queen, which is what he called me last night.

After everything I'd been through, I just wanted to be with him, not ask a million tough questions. But this morning, after a full night of sleep and a meal, a bath, and feeling clean again, I want to know. Why do these men keep calling me Princess? And why did Sebastian say I had the O'Connor heir growing in my womb?

My hand touches my belly unconsciously as I walk toward the door. It's a habit I've noticed myself doing. Every time I think of my unborn child, I touch my stomach and smile. Secrets and heirs aside, Da and Mum will be thrilled to know they'll be grandparents. Rebecca will think I'm insane until I tell her how much I've fallen for this man, the one I thought I hated but found later that all that animosity wasn't really his fault.

I hated the arrangement, the idea of it. The principle that women should be free to choose never left me, but now my heart has chosen. I want him. And I want him forever.

As I pad softly up to the living room, after nearly getting lost down the hallway, I hear sniffling and laughter. These two sounds seem strange juxtaposed, and I peek into the room before I walk fully in. Mum sits on a couch with Da next to her, Rebecca with a tissue in hand wiping her nose. Declan stands in front of them serving tea into tiny mugs with hand-painted flowers and gilded rims and handles.

It's Mum who sees me first. She rushes over to wrap her arms around me tightly, and I melt into her embrace. Da follows, walking with pride and strength toward us. Rebecca blubs and gushes, shoving her way into the center of our reunion as my father wraps all three of us ladies into his arms. I press my head against Rebecca's and close my eyes, finally at peace. I'll spare them the worst of the stories, but Da will want to know everything, I'm sure.

"I'm so glad you're back," Mum whimpers.

"Oh, Isla," Rebecca coos.

"I'm okay... Please," I mutter, feeling crushed a little. I chuckle, and one by one, they pull back.

"Come sit," Declan invites us. I'm surprised Ronan isn't here for this too since it's his home, but I do as my husband says and have a seat. He sits next to me and takes my hand and smiles.

"Well, what an adventure you've been on," Da says, but I hardly think his positive tone is the appropriate response. Still, he's a master at looking at the bright side of things.

"Yes, well, I'm here now." The question burns on my tongue, but I wait for Mum and Rebecca to fawn over me for a bit. Declan seems to sense my annoyance with them and encourages them to have some tea, which refocuses them back on doctoring their tiny mugs with cream and sugar.

I take the opportunity to address my father, whose nonchalant attitude is somewhat chilling. We've never experienced tragedy as a family, at least none that I know of, so I'm not sure if this is his normal demeanor in situations like this or if he's lost his mind. I have to know what's going on, and I can't wait any longer.

"Da," I say firmly, "what is happening?" I wring my hands in my lap and study his face as it softens and the sadness starts to creep in.

"Why, my oldest daughter is having our first grandchild. I think that's reason enough to be happy." He fiddles with his tie and glances at Declan. I don't bother to look at my husband. This is between me and my father.

"Da, tell me the truth. Why did you force me to marry Declan? Why are those men calling me Princess all the time? What does it mean that I'm carrying the O'Connor heir?"

He trades furtive glances with my mother and his shoulders stiffen, squaring. I expected him to shrink back, but this is surprising to me. He slaps the tops of his thighs and lets his hands slide to his knees where they stop.

"Aisling, I'm a proud man," he says, and suddenly, his eyes take on the same darkness that Declan's eyes get sometimes when he's angry. I glance at Mum, whose head is now hanging. "There is a lot you don't know about me."

"I think what your father is trying to tell you is that he's kept things from you for your own protection, things he should've told you a long time ago." Declan touches my leg and then lets his fingers slide into my grasp, as if knowing ahead of time that I'll need him. I look up at him with warmth and then narrow my eyes on my father.

"Tell me everything."

My father proceeds to tell me how his father built a crime organization much like the O'Rourkes'. How he traded in drugs and weapons. He tells me how when he was in his twenties, he took over for his father, running the underground crime syndicate, and how clashes with other families like the O'Rourkes led to an all-out war, a war that killed Declan's father.

When he gets to that point, I see the first sign of frailty I've ever seen come from my father. Remorse, perhaps, or grief. He goes on to tell me how after men in his organization murdered the O'Rourke chief, he was cornered and forced into a dark place he couldn't bargain his way out of. His family was turning on him. He'd allowed them to murder one of the most powerful men in the city, and now he had a debt to pay—hand over his family or just his daughter.

I sit there feeling gutted by the truths rolling out of my father's mouth. To think my entire life, he's been keeping this from me, lying for what? To give me a normal lifestyle, even when he knew I'd be forced to live with this legacy? There is no way I could ever have lived my full life without finding out. The arranged marriage was simply the catalyst for the truth to be revealed.

I'm angry, but simultaneously, I am comforted. Declan's arm comes around me, and I lean into him. Life always has a way of showing me the silver lining, and if the man to whom I'm bound continues to be the man who cares for me and protects me, then I have been the one to benefit from this whole situation.

"But an heir? What does it mean?" I say, but I already feel like I know what it means. The child in my womb will never have the future I hope for him or her.

Da nods at me and blinks, as if I'm supposed to understand, but I shake my head in confusion. "The firstborn male grandchild will be raised to take this family and lead them properly in ways I can never do." Da's voice is solemn, and I get the feeling that the choice to place that on my shoulders wasn't his, but it doesn't have to be the future. It doesn't have to be this way at all. Together, Declan and I can and will change that to make the future for our child different from what I fear, better.

31

DECLAN

I sit with Mick and his family in the cozy front room of my brother's home. We linger there for more than an hour, immersed in conversation, as Isla recounts the harrowing tale of what happened. Her voice trembles slightly as she speaks of her urgent need to escape, a desperate plea woven into her words. Each syllable is a knife twisting in my gut, especially when she describes the suffocating terror of being confined in that cold, metal container. Her vivid account only fuels the fire within me, solidifying my determination to hunt down and eliminate Sebastian O'Reilly before anyone else can intervene.

As Ronan steps into the room, his presence is immediate and commanding. He halts just inside the doorway, fixing me with a deliberate, meaningful gaze that leaves no doubt in my mind—he wants me to accompany him. I bide my time, searching for a natural lull in the lively chatter around me. When the moment feels right, I lean in close to Isla, her perfume a delicate floral note in the air. I gently place a kiss on her cheek, the warmth of her skin a comforting touch, and whisper softly, "I'll be back."

Then I rise and walk out into the hallway. Ronan isn't here, probably off to his office to wait for me. I head in that direction, tucking my tie into my suit jacket and buttoning it. After things went down, the Garda arrested more than half of the O'Reilly clan, but we know Sebastian was one of them. We also know he has his fingers in the Garda and the justice system. They won't be able to make anything stick, but that's okay.

At this moment, he's securely confined behind bars, beyond my reach, but the day they release him, I'll track him down relentlessly. In the meantime, my attention is devoted to my wife and our unborn child, ensuring their safety and well-being. I'm determined to do everything in my power to fortify our family, cultivate strong alliances, and lay the foundation for a secure and prosperous future for myself and all those around me. The gravity of my responsibilities weighs heavily upon me, fueling my resolve to protect and nurture what matters most.

I strut into Ro's office to find Finn there. He's standing opposite Ronan, who's seated behind his desk with a stack of papers in front of him. As I approach, I hear them talking, but they hush when I get within earshot. I'm sure they'll fill me in soon enough. I've learned not to be nosy and to just deal with what is given to me. It's enough to keep me busy, anyway.

"How's she doing?" Ro inquires, his voice tinged with genuine concern. I'm grateful he's pausing to recognize that Isla is an integral part of this family, cherished and deeply valued. His words carry a warmth that underscores the affection and importance we all feel for her, weaving her presence into the very fabric of our lives.

"She's shaken, but I think she'll do okay. Mick just told her everything." I fumble with my tie, desperately trying to loosen it as it feels like a constricting noose around my neck. Isla isn't a weak woman by any stretch of the imagination, but even so, I was taken aback by the composure with which she absorbed the news. Not a single flicker crossed her eyes. She didn't even blink.

"Well, Brynn is out of surgery," Ronan grumbles. "Half his liver was blown away, but he'll live, and he'll have a story to tell. I think he's learning his lesson." Ro chuckles, and Finn shifts uncomfortably.

My adversarial cousin isn't the reason I've been called into this office. I gather that much. Ronan is pissed about something and Finn seems agitated.

"If the eejit had only learned to stay in his lane and keep his mouth shut, he would've been fine." I shake my head in frustration, fingers weaving through my hair as if untangling the thoughts in my mind. The tension is palpable, and I can't help but notice the deep creases etched into Ronan's forehead, like cracks in a dry riverbed. Something's wrong, and it's more than just the words we've exchanged.

"Sit down," he says, and Finn and I obediently pull up a chair and have a seat. Ro leans forward, clasping his hands over his desk as he plants his elbows on top of it. He licks his lip and then rakes his teeth over it, pensively deciding what to say or how to start.

I tap my fingers on the arm of the chair and lean to one side. Finn crosses one leg over the other, clasping his ankle in hand. It's a long moment before Ro speaks, but what he says doesn't surprise me.

"There's a new Director of Public Prosecutions sniffing around, a young woman, sharp and talented, but with an insatiable curiosity." He steeples his fingers beneath his chin, his gaze narrowing as it settles on us both, like a predator sizing up its prey. "I'm seeking the counsel of my strategist and my enforcer on how to perceive this development. She's just graduated from law school, full of energy and determination, driven by a fiery ambition to track down and bring to light any organized crime syndicate lurking in the shadows."

"Out of the frying pan and into the fire," Finn says with a glower. "We could just take her out," he suggests, but Ronan frowns on that instantly.

"Too messy, too many layers. We'd have the whole Garda up our ass. We need to handle this tactfully, gentlemen, and quickly. After what happened down at the docks with O'Reilly, she'll be eating that case up. If he leaks anything to her about any of us, she'll be on us instantly." Ro sits back in his seat and sighs. "We have layers of safeguards, but at this point, we can't depend on any one of them. We've seen what our enemies are capable of. We have to prepare for the worst."

Finn's foot taps rhythmically against the floor, a steady beat that mirrors the determination in his nodding head. "We'll just have to dive into the research, lay a solid foundation for either Plan A or Plan B, just like we always do. We'll ensure we're fully prepared for whatever comes our way."

"I'm trusting you," Ronan tells him. Then he looks at me. "And after all this and the way you've redeemed yourself to this family, I'm trusting you too. Whatever Finn needs, you be there for him. We've got to stick together and we've got to tie up any loose ends that are still out there." Ronan stands and leans over his desk. "We can't afford any publicity, if you know what I mean."

Finn and I are acutely aware of the fragile state of the city's atmosphere, especially in the aftermath of Sebastian's reckless actions. The tension is palpable, like a thin layer of ice stretched over a deep lake, ready to crack at any moment. If our ongoing feud with him, ignited by Isla's cunning thievery, becomes the scapegoat for the relentless witch hunt spearheaded by the new prosecutor, the consequences could be dire.

The entire city, with its tangled web of familial alliances and rivalries, would turn its ire toward us. It would be like striking a match in a room filled with gasoline fumes—explosive and uncontrollable. We'd be staring down the barrel of an all-out war, with factions rising against us from every corner of the metropolis.

"Go on, then..." Ro says, his voice a mix of authority and weariness. "And Finn?"

Finn turns, catching our older brother's gaze. "Yeah, Chief?"

"I'm going to give this whole thing directly to you. I have too much on my shoulders with the alignment of our family with Mick's. Can you handle it?" Ronan's expression is serious, the weight of responsibility evident in his furrowed brow and the tight set of his jaw. The alliance is paramount, a delicate balance we must maintain, but we can't let this situation spiral out of control either.

"I got it, Ro." Finn nods, his face resolute, and we walk out into the hallway, facing an uncertain future that looms like a storm on the horizon.

But my wife is here with me, securely nestled in our temporary haven as we search for our new home. Her presence is a comforting anchor in this sea of transition. I also have a child on the way, a tiny miracle who will soon fill that home with the joyous sounds of love and laughter. Life feels like it's on an upswing, a gentle ascent toward brighter days, at least for the moment.

Printed in Great Britain
by Amazon